M─────H

FOLK
TALES

MEATH

FOLK TALES

RICHARD MARSH

The
History
Press
Ireland

First published 2013

The History Press Ireland
50 City Quay
Dublin 2
Ireland
www.thehistorypress.ie

British Library Cataloguing in Publication Data.
A catalogue record for this book is available from the British Library.

ISBN 978 1 84588 788 9

Typesetting and origination by The History Press

CONTENTS

INTRODUCTION

> The unwritten stories of Ireland mostly linger in the memories of
> old persons, and fast are they dying out; so that, in a few generations,
> all trace of them must be forgotten, since no record has been preserved,
> and few efforts have been made to place them in a shape, which might
> serve to perpetuate their poetical and imaginative character.
>
> (John O'Hanlon, *The Buried Lady: A Legend of Kilronan*, Dublin 1877)

Fortunately, many of those unwritten stories lamented by Father
O'Hanlon have since been written down and are preserved in the
National Folklore Collection at University College Dublin, which
I have plundered for some of the stories in this book. I have made little
effort to 'place them in a shape', choosing instead to present them as
I found them, leaving intact the poetical and imaginative character of
the tellers' voices. Similarly with the more literary medieval accounts of
legendary history, whose talented authors were often more economical
with words and insightful into the human condition than later writers.

Seán Ó Súilleabháin's description of the folktales and legends in his
Miraculous Plenty (1952, 2012) can be applied to many of the tales in this
book: 'not history, but attempts to fill the gaps left in history'. They are
the people's versions of history, and they often present a sharper, more
personal close-up picture of past events than official accounts. 'Old men

would be turned three times in their beds, to see if they were fit to serve in the army.' (See chapter 5.) You won't read that in the history books.

Great events and prominent figures are brought within reach when it is remembered in Duleek that King James, fleeing from the Battle of the Boyne, fell as he was crossing over a gate, giving Kingsgate its name. The more distant past is connected with the present by place-names such as Ardbraccan, founded by St Patrick's nephew Breacain next to the sacred tree of Bile Tortan, which was planted from a seed supplied by Fintan, sole sur- vivor of the Great Deluge. Mythology is literally brought to earth in Meath. Who can visit Newgrange or cross the great river of Meath, the Boyne, without being reminded of the mound's original resident, Bóann?

The traditional stories we now call myth and legend were once taught as history in Irish schools. With no documentary evidence to prove that they really happened, they were relegated to the status of folklore by modernisers in the second half of the twentieth century. At the same time, the Welsh education authorities began presenting the great mythological cycle of the *Mabinogion* as pre-history. Now Lleu Llaw Gyffes and Manawyddan vab Llyr live on in the imaginations of Welsh children and inhabit their local landscapes, as they did not do for their parents, and as those Welsh heroes' Irish counterparts, Lugh of the Long Arm and Manannán mac Lir, no longer do for this country's children.

Local stories document the successes and failures, hopes and fears of ourselves and our neighbours, and celebrate local characters and events: Meldrum the Prophet, Collier the Robber, Tom the Buddha, for example. These are preserved to a great extent in local and self-published books, such as the prolific output of the late Tommy Murray – who might have written this book if he had lived longer – and the journal of the Meath Archaeological and Historical Society, *Ríocht na Midhe*.

> Why Methe had that name: the chief King of Ireland, called Tweltactor [Tuathal Techtmar], called before him all the Kings of Ireland, and required at their hand their goodwills that he might enjoy that cuige or fifth part of Ireland, and they with one assent refused that to do; whereupon he strack off their heads, so that a body without a head is called in Irish Meythe, which name to this time resteth.
>
> (*The Book of Howth*, sixteenth century)

Long since, [Ireland] was devided into foure regions, Leinster East, Connaght West, Ulster North, Mounster South, and into a fifth plot defalked [deducted] from every fourth part, lying together in the heart of the Realme, called thereof Media, Meath.

(*A Historie of Ireland*, Edmund Campion, 1571)

In some of the old stories set in Meath, the term *Brega* – with variations *Breg, Bregia, Bregha* – is used, often preceded by '*Mag/Magh*', meaning 'plain'. It encompasses a territory bounded by Dublin, Ardee, Drogheda, and Athboy; that is, the modern County Meath with the addition of parts of Counties Louth and Dublin. Meath was designated a county in 1210 and divided into East Meath and West Meath in 1542, and over time reached its present reduced size after ceding territory to surrounding counties.

As its name suggests, Meath tends to be in the middle of things. The strongest of the Anglo-Norman barons, Hugh de Lacy, grabbed as much of its fertile fields as he could in the twelfth century and made his headquarters in Trim, where he built the finest castle of its type in Ireland.

The Hill of Tara was the political centre of Ireland for 1,000 years, until it was cursed in the sixth century AD, and it continues to be an emotional and sacred focal point. As the meeting place of heroes, kings and gods, Tara has seen the beginnings and climaxes of many mythological, legendary and historical dramas and confrontations: Lugh of the Many Talents, Midir and Étaín and Eochaid, Diarmuid and Gráinne, Fionn mac Cumhaill and Conn of the Hundred Battles, King Diarmait and St Ruadán, the 1798 Battles of Tara, Daniel O'Connell's Monster Meeting of 1843 against the Act of Union, and the anti-motorway occupation from 2007 to 2010.

The Battle of Gabhra-Achall, which took place next to Tara, signalled the end of the Fianna. The 5,200-year-old Newgrange is the most popular ancient site in Ireland. St Patrick announced the arrival of Christianity on the Hill of Slane. Trevet near Dunshaughlin has a claim for being the first Christian site in Ireland.

The Salmon of Wisdom, by which Fionn mac Cumhaill got his Thumb of Wisdom that allowed him to answer any question, was caught on the River Boyne, and the Meath Coat of Arms proudly bears that same Bradán Feasa.

The Ulster hero Cúchulainn was a native of Meath. He was born at Newgrange, and his head and right hand are buried at Tara, and the rest of him at the Hill of Slane. He remains a potent iconic figure in Irish mythological history and politics. Cúchulainn and Jesus Christ were the heroes of Patrick Pearse, the leader of the 1916 Easter Rising, because they gave their lives for their people. That is why images of the dead Cúchulainn, tied to a pillar in a seemingly deliberate evocation of Jesus on the Cross, adorn the General Post Office on O'Connell Street and Desmond Kinney's Setanta Wall off Nassau Street in Dublin.

The spelling of personal and place-names in a book of this sort is always problematic. I have generally used the most familiar forms, except in direct quotes. Two of the high kings present a particular dilemma. Diarmait mac Cerbaill was not the real name of the sixth-century high king. His father was Fergus Cerbaill for his twisted mouth – *cer-bhéal* – but the son, properly Diarmait mac Fergus Cerbaill, inherited the cognomen without the 'Fergus'. Plummer (*Lives of Irish Saints*) made the distinction: 'Diarmait son of Fergus Cerrbel (i.e Wrymouth), whom some call Diarmait son of Cerball, was king of Erin in the time of Ruadan.'

Diarmaid (following the usual spelling) mac Cerbaill was not the real name of the *seventh*-century high king, either. His father was Áed Sláine, son of Diarmait mac (Fergus) Cerbaill, but, confusingly, Diarmaid is best known by his more illustrious grandfather's name. In the text I refer to him by his correct name, Diarmaid mac Áed Sláine, to avoid ambiguity.

'Diarmuid' is spelled thus when it refers to the character in the saga The Pursuit of Diarmuid and Gráinne. The spelling of Angus/Aonghus/Oengus follows the sources.

Sources are credited within the text, dispensing with footnotes. Stories from the National Folklore Collection and the Schools collection at UCD are cited thus: (NFC volume: page) and (NFCS volume: page). A full bibliography is at the back of the book.

1

DUNSHAUGHLIN

Dunshaughlin is blessed with two approved Irish names, neither of which is unanimously accepted. Dún Seachlainn (Seachnall's Fort) is the one you see on the official sign as you enter the town, but Domhnach Seachnaill (Seachnall's Church) is preferred locally. Situated as the town is, only a few miles from Tara, it is not surprising that the doings of kings and saints feature prominently in its eventful history.

THE PROPHECIES OF ART, SON OF CONN

Art, son of Conn of the Hundred Battles, was known as Art Aonfer – 'only son' – because his only brother, Connla, set sail to the Otherworld and never returned. The famous Cormac mac Airt was the only one of Art's three sons to survive. Art had fathered the other two by his daughter, and they were killed – whether by Art for shame or by Art's brothers to prevent their inheriting the crown is not clear – one by drowning in the Boyne and the other by being thrown to a wolf. One of them, Artgen, was an ancestor of St Finbar of Cork.

Art was king of Ireland from AD 166 until he was killed in the Battle of Mag Muccrime in 195. Shortly before the battle, he was hunting alone at Duma Derglúachra, now known as Trevet (*tréde fót* – 'three sods'), 3km north of Dunshaughlin. Standing on a hunting mound – probably the earthwork in a field 1km east of Trevet – he saw angels flying up and down. The Holy Spirit infused him and bestowed the gift of prophecy on him, and he saw that he would be killed in the coming battle. He chose Trevet as his burial place, rather than the pagan cemetery at Brú na Bóinne (Newgrange), because he foresaw the coming of Christianity to Ireland and proclaimed his belief in the Holy Trinity. In a long poem, mostly in obscure language, he foretold the arrival of St Patrick.

For those reasons he is considered one of the first three Christians in Ireland. Conor mac Nessa, king of Ulster, was the first, and Art's son Cormac was the third. Conor was deemed to have received a baptism of blood, because his anger at the news of the Crucifixion expelled a brain ball lodged in his head, causing his death. (A brain ball is a missile made of the calcified brain of a slain warrior with supposed magic power.) Like his father, Cormac refused a pagan burial at the Brú.

The Metrical Dindshenchas (Lore of Place-names) confirms that Art and Cormac are not buried at Brú na Bóinne, though Conn and other kings are:

> Bright is it here, O plain of Mac ind Oc!
> wide is thy road with traffic of hundreds;
> thou hast covered many a true prince
> of the race of every king that has possessed thee.

> Thou hidest Conn the just, the hundred-fighter.
> There came not Art, highest in rank,
> round whom rode troops on the battlefield;
> he found a grave proud and lofty,
> the champion of the heroes, in Luachair Derg.
> There came not Cormac free from sorrow:
> after receiving the Truth (he affirmed it)
> he found repose above limpid Boyne
> on the shore at Rossnaree.

On the night before the Battle of Mag Muccrime in Galway, Art stayed in the house of Uilc Acha the smith, where he met Uilc Acha's daughter, Étaín. Together they made Cormac, who would later become the most celebrated of the high kings. That story is in the twelfth-century *Lebor na hUidre* (*Book of the Dun Cow*) under the title '*Fástini Airt meic Cuind*' (The Prophecies of Art son of Conn). '*Senchas na Relec*' (History of the Cemeteries), also from the *Book of the Dun Cow*, adds that when Art's body was carried to Trevet, 'if all the men of Erin tried to draw it from there, they could not, so that he was interred in that place because there was a Catholic Church to be afterwards at his burial place because the truth and the Faith had been revealed to him through his regal righteousness.'

Local historian Mickey Kenny took me to Trevet in 2010 to show me Art's grave next to an old cemetery and the ruins of a church said to be the oldest Christian site in Ireland. The story gives the location of Art's vision as '*Duma Derglúachra .i. áit hi fail Treóit indiu* – Mound of the Red Rushy Place, that is, the place where Trevet is found today'. The road from Dunshaughlin to Trevet is called the Bog Road. It passes through the townland of Redbog, which can best be described as 'red rushy'.

St Seachnall (Secundinus)

St Patrick arrived in Ireland in 432 with his nephew St Seachnall (372-447). Seachnall founded a church in Dunshaughlin and was appointed the first bishop of Dunshaughlin in 433. (Some say Seachnall arrived before or after Patrick and that they were not related.) Seachnall wrote several hymns, including one in praise of Patrick, and he transcribed another called '*Sancti, venite, Christi corpus sumite*' (Come, holy ones, take up the body of Christ) from the singing of angels. Long used as a Communion hymn, it is best known by the title of a popular nineteenth-century English translation, 'Draw Nigh and Take the Body of the Lord.' It has been described as 'that golden fragment of our ancient Irish liturgy' and is found in a late seventh-century collection called the *Antiphonary of Bangor*. Its style reveals an earlier origin, lending veracity to this story attached to the hymn, which is related in the *Irish Liber Hymnorum* (1898).

Patrick heard that Seachnall was telling people, 'Patrick would be a good man except for one thing: he doesn't preach enough about charity.' Patrick was angry at that, and he came to Dunshaughlin to confront Seachnall, who was saying Mass and had just come to the Communion. When he was told that Patrick had arrived in a temper, he left the Host on the altar and went out of the church and bowed down in front of Patrick.

Patrick drove his chariot directly at him, but God raised the ground around Seachnall so that he was not injured.

'What was that for?' asked Seachnall.

'You've been saying that I don't fulfil charity. If I don't fulfil charity I am in violation of God's commandment. But God knows that it is for charity that I don't preach it, because there will come after me to this island sons of life who will need to be supported by wealthy men. If I preach charity to these wealthy men now, they won't have anything left to give to those who come after me.'

'I didn't realise that you were not being remiss,' said Seachnall.

They made peace between them, and as they were going into the church they heard angels singing around the Host on the altar. What they were singing was the hymn beginning '*Sancti, venite, Christi corpus sumite*'.

It was partly to make it up to Patrick that Seachnall wrote a hymn about him. One day, he said to Patrick, 'When shall I write a hymn in your honour?' Patrick said, 'You don't have to do that. And besides, you don't praise the day until after the sun sets.'

It was unheard of to write a work of praise for a living person.

Seachnall said, 'I didn't say *if*, I said *when*, because I'm going to do it anyway.'

It suddenly occurred to Patrick that Seachnall didn't have long to live, and he said, 'By God, you'd better write it now.'

So Seachnall wrote the 'Hymn of St Secundinus', and when he finished it he wanted Patrick's opinion, but he didn't want Patrick to know that he was the subject. They met along the Northern Road, the Slíge Midluachra, and Seachnall said, 'I've written a hymn of praise for a certain man of God, and I'd like you to hear it.'

'Praise of the people of God is always welcome,' said Patrick. Seachnall started with the second stanza, '*Beata Christi custodit mandata in omnibus*' (he keeps Christ's holy commandments in all things) because the first stanza has Patrick's name in it. The hymn begins with '*Audite, omnes amantes Deum*' (Listen, all lovers of God) and each following stanza starts with the succeeding letter of the alphabet: '*Constans … Dominus … Electa …*'

When he reached '*Maximus namque in regno coelorum vocabitur*' (for he will be called the greatest in the Kingdom of Heaven) Patrick stopped him and asked, 'How can you describe a man as "greatest in the Kingdom of Heaven"?'

'It doesn't mean that he *is* the greatest in Heaven. It means that in Heaven he will be *called* greatest, because he is the greatest among the men of his race here on earth, and he will be so recognised in Heaven.'

When Seachnall reached the final stanza – 'May we always sing Patrick's praises' – Patrick thanked him for the tribute. Seachnall asked him for a poet's fee.

'As many sinners as there are hairs in your cloak,' said Patrick, 'shall go to Heaven for singing the hymn.'

'That's not enough,' said Seachnall.

'Then I'll give you this: everyone who recites it going to sleep and waking up will go to Heaven.'

'But the hymn is long. Not everyone will be able to commit it to memory.'

'The virtue of the hymn,' said Patrick, 'is in the last section. Whosoever of the men of Ireland shall recite the three last stanzas, or the three last lines, or the three last words, just before death, with a pure mind, his soul will be saved.'

'Thanks be to God,' Seachnall said.

St Colman Ela, one of the three great Colmans of Meath, founded a monastery in County Offaly. One day, he recited '*Audite, omnes*' three times in a row in his dining hall in the presence of St Patrick. A man standing nearby complained at the choice and said, 'Have we no other prayer that we could recite except this?' Patrick took this as a personal affront and stalked out of the room in anger.

A century later, Cainnech (St Canice of Kilkenny) was in a boat on the sea when he saw a black cloud of devils flying overhead.

'Stop here on your way back,' he called to them. On their return they reported that they had gone to collect the soul of a certain wealthy man.

'He sang two or three stanzas of *Audite, omnes*, and we thought it sounded more like a satire than a hymn of praise, but it defeated us.'

LOUGH GABHAIR (LAGORE)

According to the *Annals of the Four Masters*, Lough Gabhair, the now-dried up lake in the townland of Lagore just outside Dunshaughlin, was formed in 1513 BC.

The *Rennes Dindshenchas* tells how Lough Gabhair got its name. Eochaid Cind Mairc (Horsehead), king of Munster, sent two white mares to Enna Aignech, king of Tara, as tribute, but they were drowned in the lake when a stallion chased them, hence 'Loch Gabar' (Lake of Steeds). (*Gabar/gabor* can also mean 'goat'.)

Blathmac, son of Áed Sláine, was king of Brega, part of Meath, before he and his brother Diarmaid shared the kingship of Ireland from 657 to 664. Blathmac's royal seat was a newly built crannóg (a manmade defensive island residence) in Lough Gabhair, one of the largest – 520ft in circumference – and richest crannógs in Ireland.

In 647 or 651, the Leinster champion Maelodrán killed Blathmac's two sons at a watermill in County Westmeath. (See chapter 10 for St Ultán's epitaph on the boys.) Blathmac threatened the Leinstermen with invasion unless they gave up Maelodrán to him, but Maelodrán told his people not to worry, because he was going to surrender to Blathmac.

He didn't surrender. Instead, he went to Lough Gabhair at night, took a boat across to the crannóg, and waited outside Blathmac's house. Eventually, Blathmac came out to 'bend his knees', as a twelfth-century manuscript delicately puts it, or to 'sit by himself', as another blushingly hints. In the darkness, and probably half-asleep and half-drunk, Blathmac could barely make out the form of Maelodrán and mistook him for one of his guards.

'You there! Hold my sword,' the king commanded.

Maelodrán did so. When Blathmac had finished relieving himself, he ordered Maelodrán to hand him something to wipe his bottom. Maelodrán gave him a bunch of stinging nettles.

'Ow. I'm burned, I'm wounded. That was no friend who did that. Who are you?'

'I'm Maelodrán, who is just after killing your two sons. And now ...', he held Blathmac's own sword to his throat, '... I have you in my power.'

'That's true. Can we go into the house and talk about this?'

The upshot was that Blathmac gave Maelodrán a horse, a suit of clothes, a brooch, and free passage back to Leinster, and thereafter they fought together against their common enemies.

The *Annals of the Four Masters* report that in 848 Cinaedh, king of North Brega, rebelled against the high king, Maelseachlainn, and plundered Lough Gabhair and burned it 'so that it was level with the ground'. Then he burned the oratory of Trevet, 'within which were three score and two hundred persons'. The following year, Maelseachlainn and Tigernach, king of Lough Gabhair and South Brega, drowned Cinaedh in the River Nanny (described as 'a dirty streamlet') in revenge.

A NEW HEROINE

Marvel Comics super-heroine Shamrock – real name Molly Fitzgerald – was born in Dunshaughlin, date unknown, and made her first public appearance in Marvel's *Contest of Champions #1* in June 1982. She is costumed in two-tone green with shamrocks, and her super-power is a protective aura that causes 'random improbabilities' to protect her when she is in trouble: in other words, she embodies the luck of the Irish. She's retired now and works as a hair stylist. Folklorists of the future will undoubtedly include her in their dictionaries.

2

SLANE

The twelfth-century *Dindshenchas* (Lore of Place-names), compiled
from earlier sources, gives us several choices for the derivation of the
name of Slane:

Rudraige and 150 men were chasing a wild boar at the Hill of
Slane. The boar killed fifty hunters and broke Rudraige's spears. His
son, Rossa, came to his rescue and turned the boar away without his
spears being broken. As a result, the name of *Sliabh Slan-ga* (the Hill
of the Whole Spear) was given to the hill.

Or, Slanga, son of Partholon, was buried there. Slanga was the first
healer in Ireland, and the Irish word for 'health' is *slán*. Low mounds
near the college on the hill are believed to be the grave of Partholonians
killed in a plague.

Or, Slaine, Leinster king of the Fir Bolg, was buried there.

St Patrick gave Slane its main claim to fame. It is generally agreed
that he was appointed bishop by the Pope and arrived in Ireland in
AD 432. In Wicklow they say he landed at Arklow or Wicklow Town,
but the people threw stones at him and he left. He came up the coast
and stopped at Swords, looking for fish. He found none and went to
St Patrick's Island off Skerries and then on to the mouth of the Nanny
at Laytown, where again he found nothing. He cursed all three places,
and so they are said to be unfruitful.

He arrived at Drogheda in 433 and made his way up the Boyne. Having served many years as a slave, Patrick was able to speak Irish and knew the customs of the land. He was aware that all fires had to be extinguished on the eve of the First of May and that the druids would light a fire in front of the king on the Hill of Tara to celebrate the first day of summer. (As late as the nineteenth century, farmers were reluctant to light fires early on May Day, for fear that something bad would happen to their cattle.) So Patrick lit a bonfire on the Hill of Slane to attract attention, knowing that it would be visible from Tara 10 miles (16km) away.

King Laoghaire saw the fire, which illuminated all of Meath. His druids told him that if the fire was not quenched that night, the person who had lit it would have the kingdom of Ireland forever. Laoghaire led his warriors to Slane, but they didn't arrive until daylight. The druids said to Laoghaire, 'Don't go to him, lest it seem that you are paying him honour. Make him come to you, but let none of your people show him respect.'

When Patrick saw them with their horses and chariots, he sang a verse from the Book of Psalms (19:8): 'Some trust in chariots, and some in horses, but we will call upon the name of the Lord our God.' One of Laoghaire's druids, Erc, stood to show respect and later converted. When Patrick founded the church on the Hill of Slane, he made Erc the bishop. His grave is still to be seen in the graveyard: it's the one with two rough triangular stones at either end.

Another druid, Lochru, insulted the Christian faith, and Patrick prayed, 'Let this impious one, who is blaspheming Thy name, be destroyed.'

Demons raised the druid in the air and dropped him so that his head struck a stone, and he was turned into ashes.

Laoghaire ordered his men to attack Patrick, and Patrick quoted Psalm 67:2: 'May God arise, and may his enemies be scattered.'

Immediately darkness came over the sun. The earth shook, and thunder rumbled overhead. The horses panicked and ran, and the chariots were scattered as far as Slíab Moduirn, south of Castleblayney in Monaghan, over 30 miles away. The warriors began fighting one another, and fifty were killed as a result of Patrick's curse. Only three were left with Patrick on the hill: Laoghaire, his queen, whose name was Angass, and a serving man of the king.

Angass said, 'O just and mighty man, don't kill the king. He will submit to you and do what you wish.'

Laoghaire knelt before Patrick and pretended to accept the Faith. Then he took Patrick aside and said, 'Follow me to Tara, so that I can profess my belief before the men of Ireland.'

He instructed his people to set ambushes for Patrick and his eight followers between Slane and Tara, but Patrick suspected a trap. He blessed his followers and a cloak of invisibility covered them. It was on this occasion that he made the popular prayer called 'The Deer's Cry' or 'The *Lorica* (Breastplate) of St Patrick', which is best known for the verse that begins 'Christ with me, Christ before me ...' All the would-be ambushers saw was a group of eight wild deer, with a fawn – Patrick's favourite disciple, young Benen (Benignus) – bringing up the rear. When they arrived at Tara, Laoghaire invited Patrick to a meal. A druid named Lucatmael poured poison into Patrick's cup of ale, but Patrick noticed it. He blessed the cup and turned it upside down, and the poison flowed out, leaving the ale, which Patrick drank.

Lucatmael then challenged Patrick: 'Let's work wonders together to see which of us is the stronger.'

'So be it,' said Patrick.

Lucatmael caused snow to cover the plain to the height of a man's shoulders.

'Now let's see you take it away,' said Patrick.

'I can't take it away until this time tomorrow.'

'By God, I can.'

Patrick blessed the plain, and the snow disappeared without the help of sun or rain. Then Lucatmael brought darkness over the plain, so heavy it could be felt.

'Now take away the darkness, if you can,' Patrick said.

'I can't do that until this time tomorrow.'

Patrick blessed the plain, and the sun dispelled the darkness.

Laoghaire suggested a trial by fire: Benen to be placed in the part of a hut made of dry timber wearing Lucatmael's cloak, and Lucatmael to be placed in the part of the same hut made of green wood wearing Patrick's cloak. The fire was lit. The green-wood part and Lucatmael were incinerated, but Patrick's cloak was not burned, and the dry-wood part and Benen were not touched by the flames, but Lucatmael's cloak was destroyed.

Everyone present professed belief in the Christian god and was baptised, except Laoghaire. He again pretended that he believed, but Patrick knew he wasn't sincere, and he foretold that no son of Laoghaire would be king. The queen, Angass, asked Patrick not to curse the child who was then in her womb, Lugaid. Patrick said he would hold off the curse until Lugaid opposed him.

One day Patrick and his band of clerics visited the queen at Tara, and she invited them for a meal. Lugaid ate so fast that a large piece of bread lodged in his throat. Patrick gave him milk to wash the bread down, but it made the bread swell up, and Lugaid choked to death. Patrick prayed *crosfhighil* (cross-vigil: kneeling with his arms spread in the form of a cross) for three days and three nights. St Michael the Archangel appeared in the form of a dove, reached into the dead boy's throat and pulled the bread out. Lugaid immediately came back to life.

When Angass found out that her son was alive, she came and thanked Patrick profusely. Patrick explained what had happened and told her that credit should go to St Michael. The queen then promised to donate one sheep from each of her flocks every year and a portion of every meal she ate to the poor, and she ordered that every Christian in Ireland should do the same. This is said to be the origin of some Michaelmas (29 September) traditions, for example, the Michaelmas Bannock made with sheep's milk. Alternatively, Patrick commanded that everyone should set aside a tenth portion of food for the King of the Clouds and a morsel for Michael.

Lugaid was high king from 482 until 507, when he mocked the then-deceased Patrick by pointing at a church and saying, 'Is that not the church of the cleric who said no son of my father would ever be king?' He was instantly struck and killed by a bolt of lightning.

The King's Road to Slane

Looking south towards Dublin from the Hill of Slane, or poring over a map, you can't help but notice that the road from Dublin to Slane is unusually straight. It wasn't always that way. Like most country roads, it zigzagged logically to connect centres of population. But an Act of Parliament in 1815 ordered that the road be repaired and straightened at a cost of some £7,000, about €23 million today. Why?

Elizabeth Denison (1769–1861) married the Viscount of Slane, Henry Conyngham, in 1794, but reportedly set her sights on the Prince Regent, who became King George IV in 1820. She eventually became his mistress – one of six – in 1819.

In Slane it is said that the road was straightened so that George could travel quickly from Dublin to Slane to confer with the by then Marchioness Conyngham, presumably to ask her advice on matters of State.

THE FOUR SISTERS

This is the name given to the four identical eighteenth-century Georgian houses at the crossroads in Slane, which is known as the Square but is actually an octagon because the houses are set at an angle to the streets.

The story goes that a man had four daughters who did not get on well with one another, and he built the houses for them so that they would have to look at their sisters' houses every time they came out the front door. It has been reported that the current occupants of the houses are a Catholic priest, a Protestant minister, a Jewish rabbi, and a Muslim imam. There are some people who say that, 'contrary to popular myth', neither of those stories is true.

However, C.E.F. Trench, in his invaluable forty-eight-page guide, *Slane* (1976), after affirming, 'In fact, there never were four such ladies,' says:

> Another story is that they were built for the representatives of religion, medicine, law and order, but this too can be scotched, although in fact in the latter part of the nineteenth century they were indeed occupied by the priest, the doctor, the magistrate and the constabulary.

'OVER FORK OVER'

In 1040 in Ayrshire, farmer Malcolm Friskin was forking hay onto a haystack, when a horseman galloped into his farmyard and cried, 'Hide me. Some men are trying to kill me.'

Malcolm told the man to jump into the haystack, and he started to throw hay over him, but not quickly enough for the fugitive.

'Over, fork over,' he implored urgently, meaning fork more hay and faster. Malcolm did so, and when a troop of horsemen arrived in hot pursuit they were not able to find their quarry. It turned out that the man Malcolm Friskin had saved was Malcolm Canmore, Prince of Scotland, son of the King Duncan assassinated by Macbeth, who was now king. Malcolm was the rightful king, and Macbeth was trying to kill him to keep his place on the throne secure.

Seventeen years later, when Prince Malcolm killed Macbeth and became King Malcolm III, he remembered his saviour and rewarded him with the Thanedom (like a Barony) of Cunningham.

That part of the story is labelled 'a charming legend, but …' But history goes on to say that the same family settled in Ireland in 1611 and took over the original Slane Castle from the Fleming family. The present castle dates from 1785.

But the durable 'charming legend' was commemorated in the sign that used to hang in front of the Conyngham Arms Hotel on the main street of Slane. The motto 'Over Fork Over' was illustrated with a shakefork, a crude pitchfork made from the forked branch of a tree, with the Latin inscription *Quis separabit* – literally 'who will separate (us)?' – which is understood to declare loyalty to the king.

Which leads to an alternative legend. The Cunninghams were on the side of King Robert Bruce when he was fighting against the English. They concealed themselves in wagons covered with hay and thus arrived unchallenged at the gate of the English-held Linlithgow Castle. They leapt out and overpowered the guards, throwing them into the air with their shakeforks and shouting 'Over, fork over,' allowing the Bruce army to take the castle.

I was idly leafing through the 1849 issue of *Sporting Review*, when I noticed that the three-year-old chestnut colt Over-fork-over, by Slane out of Partiality, won a handicap by half a length at 5-1 on 26 October at Newmarket. Slane was a son of the famous Royal Oak, for whom the Group One Prix Royal-Oak, the French equivalent of the St Leger, was named. Slane won seven of his ten starts as a four-year-old and became a leading sire in England. Among his progeny was Railway Plate winner Marquis of Conyngham.

3

THE GORMANSTON FOXES

The Preston family arrived in Meath from Preston in Lancashire in the fourteenth century and soon became prominent 'Old English' Catholics. The title Viscount was awarded to the family in 1478 as the premier viscountcy in Ireland.

The story of the Gormanston foxes has been spread far and wide by students from Gormanston College, the Franciscan secondary school at Gormanston Castle near the border of County Dublin. It is also part of local oral tradition, and has found its way into collections of folklore and legends. But little-known first-hand reports by reliable witnesses raise an eerily charming legend to the status of family history.

The 1926 *Complete Peerage* sums up the story in the entry for the Preston family of Gormanston Castle: 'When the head of the house dies, and for some days before, the foxes leave all the neighbouring coverts, and collect at the door of the Castle.'

Everyone who has heard the story knows the reason for this. At some unspecified time in the distant past – some say the seventeenth century – a Viscount Gormanston rescued a vixen and her young litter from the hounds during a hunt. In gratitude for this act of kindness, when the viscount died, all the foxes in the district gathered on the lawn of the castle and howled with grief. The foxes did not attempt to molest the farmyard fowl, and the dogs of the house left the foxes in peace. This ritual continued for many generations.

In fact, that was the 12th Viscount, who died in 1860, according to Eileen Gormanston (Eileen Butler Preston), wife of the 15th Viscount. In her memoirs, *A Little Kept* (1953), she says that when she was ill with a high fever following the birth of her first child, her nurse told her

there were two animals larger than cats sitting under her window. Lady Gormanston said, 'Oh, I hope they're not foxes,' and told the legend to the nurse, who quickly assured her that 'the one thing they most certainly were not was foxes, and that, in any case, they had now run away.'

Following the death of Jenico William Joseph Preston, the 14th Viscount, in October 1907, the April 1908 issue of *The New Ireland Review* carried statements by members of the Preston family and household staff.

Mrs Lucretia Farrell, daughter of the 13th Viscount, said:

> On the day before my grandfather, Jenico, 12th Viscount Gormanston, died, the foxes came in pairs (an unusual thing) into the demesne from all the country round; they sat under his bedroom window, which was on the ground floor, and howled and barked all night, although constantly driven away only to return.
>
> Next morning we found them crouching about in the grass in front and around the house. In those days there were many hares in front of the house, and the foxes merely wandered through them and the same amongst the poultry; and even when driven away they only crouched down before one.

Lady Gormanston said:

> At the death of Edward, the 13th Viscount [in 1876], the foxes were also there. He had been rather better one day, but the foxes appeared, barking under the window, and he died that night contrary to expectation.

The coachman, Anthony Delahan, described his experience on the night of 28 October 1907, after the 14th Viscount died in Dublin earlier that day:

> At about 8 o'clock, I saw two foxes in the chapel ground and five or six more round the front of the house and several more in the cloisters, which were circling round in a ring, crying all the time. I saw them continuously from then till about 11 o'clock when I went to bed.

Richard Preston, son of the 14th Viscount, reported what happened two nights later:

> At about 10 p.m., I went down to the chapel at Gormanston Castle to watch by the remains of my father. ... From the outside came a continuous and insistent snuffling noise, accompanied by whimperings and scratching at the door ... It suddenly flashed across me that these must be the foxes. I accordingly went to the side door of the chapel and opened it suddenly. The night was very dark, but from the many candles within the chapel there flashed a broad beam of light through the wide open door. In the very centre of this beam of light, sitting on the gravel path within four feet of where I stood, was a full grown fox. Just in the shadow, sitting close up against the walls of the chapel, was another. ... Neither of the two which I saw attempted to move until I left the chapel and took a step towards them. They then *walked* quietly off into the shadow. I returned to the chapel, closed the door, and went across to the other door opposite the altar. As soon as I opened it I saw two more foxes, one walking across the door about nine or ten feet away, the other sitting against the wall so close that I could have touched him with my foot. ... the noise of whining and sniffling was that of a considerable number ... It continued without intermission till 5 a.m., when it ceased suddenly.

Elizabeth, Countess of Fingall, said in her memoirs, *Seventy Years Young* (1937), that the foxes were already in mourning at Gormanston before word came from Dublin that the viscount had died. Her husband was hunting that day and a man told him he might as well go home: 'Every fox in Meath is at Gormanston.' Another account says that foxes also mourned at the house in Dublin where the viscount died.

Jenico Edward Joseph, the 15th Viscount, served in the First World War. His wife, Eileen, received a letter saying that he had been killed in action, but she didn't believe he was dead, as the foxes had not put in an appearance at the house. A few weeks later, she learned there had been a mistake, and her husband was still alive. The foxes gathered at Gormanston for him when he died in 1925, as they did for Jenico

William Richard, the 16th Viscount, who was killed at Dunkirk in 1940. The present (17th) Viscount, Jenico Nicholas Dudley, succeeded to the title at the age of seven months.

John Campbell-Kease (*Tribute to an Armorist*, 2000) reports:

> A distinguished Irish lady, who was living near Gormanston at the time, told me that one of the villagers came into her parents' house one morning in June 1940 and said, 'Something has happened to Lord Gormanston, the foxes were barking all night long.' The news that the 16th Viscount had been killed in action in France came through shortly after.

The Gormanston family crest shows a fox 'pleasantly passant', and in the coat of arms is a fox 'aggressively rampant'.

The Preston family sold the property in 1946, and it has been a secondary school since 1950.

4

THE TELTOWN FAIRS

There are four royal sites in the ancient province of Meath: Uisneach, Tara, Tlachtga (the Hill of Ward near Athboy), and Tailtiu (Teltown, between Navan and Kells). '*Teltown* is a very vulgar modern corruption, supported by no respectable authority,' according to John O'Donovan in his 1836 *Ordnance Survey Letters Meath*.

Gatherings were held at these sites at significant times of the year: Tlachtga and Tara at Samhain (November Eve, with Tlachtga serving as prelude), Tailtiu at Lughnasa (August), Uisneach at Bealtaine (May Eve). Uisneach is in the present-day Westmeath; the others are in Meath.

Lugh was the son of Cian of the Tuatha Dé Danann and Ethlinn, daughter of Fomorian leader Balor, who Lugh killed in the Second Battle of Moytura. He is known as Lugh Lámhfhada (of the Long Arm) and Lugh Samildánach (of the Many Talents). He was the father of Cúchulainn and a cousin of Fionn mac Cumhaill. Lugh's human foster mother, Tailtiu, was the daughter of the king of Spain. She married Eochu, son of Erc, king of Ireland. When she died as a result of her labours in clearing trees to make the Plain of Meath, he instituted the Aenach Tailteann, the Teltown Fair, in her honour.

A fair with gold, with silver, with games, with music of chariots, with adornment of body and of soul by means of knowledge and eloquence.

A fair without wounding or robbing of any man, without trouble, without dispute, without reaving, without challenge of property, without suing, without law-sessions, without evasion, without arrest.

A fair without sin, without fraud, without reproach, without insult, without contention, without seizure, without theft, without redemption.
(From *The Metrical Dindshenchas*)

According to *Rennes Dindshenchas* 99:

Now that was fifteen hundred years before the birth of Christ; and the fair was held by every king who took Ireland until the coming of Patrick; and there were five hundred fairs in Tailtiu from Patrick till the *Dub-oenach* 'Black Assembly' of Donchad son of Fland son of Maelsechlainn [when Muircheartach son of Niall challenged High King Donchad to a battle in 925]. ... There were three taboos for Tailtiu: crossing without alighting, looking over the left shoulder when leaving, and throwing things frivolously after sunset.

Laurence Ginnell, in *The Brehon Laws: A Legal Handbook* (1894) records that:

Aenach means, first, an assembly; second, a hill, from assemblies meeting on hills; third, a cattle-fair, from such fairs springing up where aenachs once were held. Wherever an aenach was held a fair sprang up, but the latter was purely a consequential and collateral adjunct to the former. The aenach proper was an assembly of all the people of a district, without distinction of rank, and apparently without distinction of clan.

The Celtic Milesians arrived from Spain on Thursday, 30 April 1699 BC. Tailtiu was the site of the decisive battle between them and the ruling Tuatha Dé Danann. The Milesians, an Iron Age people with iron weapons, defeated the Bronze Age Dananns. They divided Ireland equally between them: the Milesians took the upper half and gave the Dananns the half under the ground. The Dananns' chief wizard,

Manannán mac Lir, taught them how to come and go in the natural and manmade hills. Before the battle, the Danann queens, Éire, Fodhla and Banba, each asked the Milesians to name the country after her if they won, which they did. Éire became the usual name, and Fodhla and Banba are still used as poetic names. Ollamh Fodhla, the Philosopher King buried in Cairn T at Loughcrew, codified the laws of Ireland and introduced the Feast of Tara, and the northernmost point of the country, in Donegal, is called Banba's Crown.

The last old-style Aonach Tailteann was celebrated in 1168 by Roderic O'Connor, the last high king, to be replaced by the more secular Teltown Fairs. These were social gatherings with horse racing and other sports, which continued until the eighteenth century and then were revived briefly in the early 1900s. They were famous (or infamous) for the Teltown Marriages, in which a couple could enter into a trial marriage. If it didn't work out after a year and a day, they could dissolve the union by standing in the spot where they had been married, turn their backs on each other and walk away to the north and the south.

WONDERS AT TAILTIU

St Ciarán the Younger, who founded Clonmacnoise in 546, wanted to study at the monastery at Clonard under St Finnian, but his family was too poor to afford tuition fees. He asked his parents if he could take one of their cows as payment. 'Go through the herds,' his father told him, 'and whatever follows you, take it.' A dun cow, the Odar Ciaráin, followed him to Clonard, and she used to give twelve measures of milk every day, enough for all of the Twelve Apostles of Ireland.

When Ciarán finished his studies and set out on his travels, he ordered that when the cow died her hide should be sent to him. After he founded Clonmacnoise, the hide was preserved there, and Ciarán said, 'Every soul that shall go out of its body on the hide of the Dun shall not be punished in Hell.' Later, the hide was used to make the famous twelfth-century collection of stories, the *Book of the Dun Cow*.

St Ciarán was at an Aonach Tailteann when a woman accused her husband, Abacuc, of infidelity, which he denied. She said she would

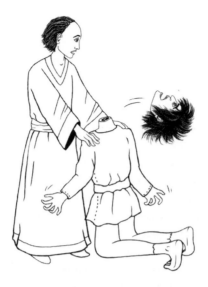

only believe his denial if he swore his innocence under the hand of St Ciarán. So he swore under Ciarán's hand, but he was lying, and where the saint's hand had touched his neck an ulcerous tumour appeared, and his head fell off. He then walked around the fair headless, and this was one of the wonders of that Teltown Fair.

Ciarán took him to Clonmacnoise to look after him, and many years later a woman was brought to the man, and 'he made it up with her, and in due course she bore him a son.' (It's not clear, but context suggests that the woman was his wife.) It is said that the Sogain, a subset of the Picts, of Meath are this man's descendants. Sogain surnames are Mannion, Manning, McWard, O'Scurry, Scarry, O'Lennan, O'Casin, O'Gilla, O'Maigin, Duggan and O'Dugevan.

A wonder of another Aonach Tailteann was the appearance of three ships sailing in the air in the time of Donall, son of Murrough. An entry in the *Annals of the Four Masters* reports that in AD 743: 'Ships, with their crews, were plainly seen in the sky this year.' The Irish Nennius (xxiii) gives details: 'Congalach, son of Mailmithigh, was at the fair of Taillten on a certain day, and he perceived a ship in the air. He saw one of the crew cast a dart at a salmon. The dart fell down in the presence of the fair, and a man came out of the ship after it. When his head came down it was caught by a man from below, upon which the man from above said, "I am being drowned."

"Let him go," said Congalach, and he was allowed to come up, and he went away from them, swimming in the air, afterwards.'

NIALL FROSSACH'S TRUE JUDGMENT

Niall Frossach was king of Tara from 763 until 770 or 777, when he resigned and went to Iona for a life of meditation and prayer. He died there in 778. He was regarded as a particularly righteous king. Signs of 'righteousness' were health among his subjects, agricultural abundance, good weather, peace, just rule, and, especially, true judgment. Propitiously, three showers fell when he was born: silver, honey and wheat. (Frossach = showery.) The silver was used to decorate the holy shrines.

There was a great famine at the beginning of Niall's reign. In the company of seven bishops, he prayed to God that if His wrath could not otherwise be appeased, God should take Niall to Himself so that his subjects would be saved. Immediately a shower of silver fell from Heaven. Niall rejoiced but said that the silver would not be useful in relieving the famine. He prayed again and a shower of honey came down. He gave thanks and then a shower of wheat covered all the fields, enough to support not only Ireland but a great many other kingdoms as well.

This story, from the twelfth-century *Book of Leinster*, illustrates Niall's true judgment.

A woman carrying a baby approached him at the Aonach Tailteann with a request.

'Please use your true judgment to tell me who is the father of my son, for I don't know. I have not lain with a man for many years.'

Niall was silent for a moment, then asked, 'Have you ever sported with a woman?'

She admitted that she had.

'The truth,' said Niall, 'is that the woman had just been with a man, and the semen he left in her was transferred to your womb while you were tumbling around with her. That man is the father of your baby, and you will have to find out who he is.'

5

THE BLACK
PIG'S DYKE

In Riverstown townland, 1.2km west of the Hill of Tara, are two double-banked earthworks. One is 700m long and the other is about half that length. There is another similar earthwork in western County Meath between Kinnegad and the Hill of Down.

Similar monuments are found all over Ireland, variously called the Worm's Ditch, the Dane's (or Danes') Cast, the Duncladh, and most often the Black Pig's Dyke. Archaeologists refer to them as 'travelling earthworks'. Some appear to be defensive structures, as is the case with the 100 BC Dorsey Entrenchment in County Armagh, where burnt sharpened oak posts were found pointing south against an expected invasion. 'The Cattle Raid of Cooley', which tells about an invasion of Ulster by the rest of Ireland, is set about that time. Others seem to be holding pens, possibly for rustled cattle, or boundary markers, and some archaeologists suggest a ritual significance. One theory is that the discontinuous line of earthworks along the shifting Ulster border as it was 2,000 years ago, and all dated to about that time, combines ritual and defence. There used to be a pub in that border area, on the R189 south of Newbliss in County Monaghan, called The Black Kesh; *céis* is an Irish word for pig.

In a paper delivered to the Royal Irish Academy in 1909, W.F. de Vismes Kane described how he was working on the Ordnance Survey in Monaghan when his 'attention was especially arrested by the vestiges of a great embankment and ditch'. He found several more segments in the vicinity. The ditches were generally about 20ft deep measured from the top of the embankments and situated so that they could defend against an attack from the south.

> The names attached to the earthwork are strange. 'The Black Pig's Race', or 'Rut', or 'Valley' (*Gleann na Muice Duibhe*), and the 'Worm Ditch,' or 'Dyke'. The legends attached to the former name are very grotesque; and their main drift is that a magical pig, originally from Meath, raged westward through Ireland, and tore up this deep furrow with its snout.
>
> The worm or *peist* was a dragon whose folds left the sinuous track over hill and dale … their value mainly consists in their almost universal reference to Meath as connected somehow with the origin of the ditch; as also the fact of supernatural agencies being introduced to explain its origin, which is a token of great antiquity.

Those 'grotesque' legends take many forms. This is the version I tell in schools, with the introduction: 'Do you want to hear a story about a *bad* teacher?' The answer is always a resounding 'Yes', with a mischievous-guilty glance at the teacher, who always – so far – takes it in good humour.

> There was once a schoolmaster who had the magic power to change people into animals by tapping them on the head with his wand. One day at the break, he changed the boys into hounds and the girls into hares, and the hounds chased the hares around the schoolyard until the end of the break, and then he changed them back into boys and girls.
>
> At least they got a lot of exercise, but the children didn't like being changed into animals, and when they got home and their parents asked them why they were so tired, they told them what the schoolmaster had done. The parents didn't like that, either, and they went to see a wise old woman to ask her advice. She told the parents what to do, and the parents told the children.
>
> The following day, when the schoolmaster was about to change the boys and girls into hounds and hares, they asked him, 'Master, can you change yourself into an animal?'

'Of course I can. What kind of animal do you want me to change into?'

'A pig.'

So he tapped himself on the head with his magic wand and turned into a pig. But when he went to change himself back into the schoolmaster, he couldn't. He had forgotten that pigs don't have fingers, and so he couldn't pick up the wand to tap himself on the head.

He was so angry that the children had tricked him that he ran all over Ireland, digging trenches with his tusks. So now where you see two ditches side by side, that is when he was running in a straight line with both tusks in the ground, and where you see only one ditch, that is when he was turning and had only one tusk in the ground.

He ran through Athlone and, as he was crossing the bridge over the Shannon, a woman hit him on the head with a big wooden hammer and killed him.

In other versions of the story the schoolmaster turned the children into pigs, and it was they who made the Black Pig's Dykes. In his paper, de Vismes Kane brought up two ancient legends that he felt might have been the origins of the Black Pig story.

In the first, three sisters married three men, but the women's mother disapproved of the matches and changed all six into pigs. They stayed with

Buchet the innkeeper in Wicklow, then with Aonghus in Brú na Bóinne, then with Drebrenn, the sister of Queen Maeve of Connacht. Eventually, they were incarcerated in the Cave of Cruachan, from which they escaped to ravage Ireland for seven years until they were killed. The other story is known as The Death of the Sons of Tuirenn, one of the Three Sorrowful Tales of Ireland. Cian, the father of Lugh of the Long Hand, transformed himself into a pig to escape an attack by the Sons of Tuirenn but was killed.

De Vismes Kane cites several other stories from various parts of Ireland. In many of them the schoolmaster or druid comes from somewhere along the Boyne near Drogheda, and the pig is killed while crossing the Shannon. De Vismes Kane cites this as evidence that the Black Pig's Dyke, at least in the Meath-Monaghan-Cavan area, reflects the border between Leinster and Ulster as it was before Tuathal Techtmar appropriated what is now Louth, North County Dublin, and parts of other counties and added them to the present County Meath to form the royal province of Meath in the first century AD.

Folklore collector P.J. Gaynor heard a version from his father, James, who lived in Edengora and died in 1926 at the age of 81. It includes the frequent motif of a great battle associated with the Black Pig. This tale begins in Athlone. One of the pupils has paid close attention to the words of the schoolmaster's spell, and he changes the master into a pig and the boys and girls into hounds, and the hounds chase the pig to the gates of Drogheda, where they kill him. The course of the chase is known as the Valley of the Black Pig, and it runs through Edengora, between Bailieborough and Kilmainhamwood. According to James:

> There was an old prophecy that 'when the war would come to Ireland it would be at its worst in the Valley of the Black Pig.' The 'greatest slaughter of all' would take place there, and the old prophecy said 'for those living in the Valley of the Black Pig, happy would the man be who burned his house and lay in the ashes.' ... When the war would come to Ireland 'a horseman would come riding like the wind to give warning to the people. Old men would be turned three times in their beds, to see if they were fit to serve in the army.'

> (NFC 792:392-95)

6

THE BATTLE
OF THE BOYNE

George Story is considered the most important authority on the struggle between the Catholic James and the Protestant William for the crowns of England, Scotland and Ireland. He was present on the Williamite side at the Battle of the Boyne in 1690 as a regimental chaplain. In his *A true and impartial history* … (1691) he reported that a Jacobite gunner …

> … fired a piece which killed us two horses and a man, about a hundred yards above where the King [William] was, but immediately came a second which had almost been a fatal one, for it grazed upon the bank of the river, and in the rising slanted upon the King's right shoulder, took out a piece of coat, and tore the skin and flesh …

In his 1826 autobiography, *Recollections*, popular Irish playwright John O'Keeffe (1747–1833) recounted what happened next:

> In 1765, at Sligo, I had seen John O'Brien, who had served at the Battle of the Boyne. He was a fine old man, and told me many interesting and circumstantial anecdotes relative to that day; one, that a gunner [apparently the same one who had wounded William] told King James that at that very precise moment his gun

was so pointed, he could, at a twinkle, end the dispute for the three crowns; but James forbad him; and the nephew and son-in-law were thus saved.

Patrick Kennedy gives that story his typical colourful spin in *Modern Irish Anecdotes* (1872):

> Burke, the cannonier, catching a sight of William on the rising ground beyond the river, adjusted his piece, so as to put him out of all worldly care and pain, and cried out to King James, who was standing near, 'I'm going to present your Majesty with three crowns. I have William covered.'
>
> 'Oh, you wretch!' answered James, striking the cannon angrily with his cane, 'would you make my daughter a widow!'
>
> Burke was anything but pleased with the royal speech.
>
> 'D—— a shot,' he muttered to himself, 'will I ever fire for you again after this battle, *Shamus a choka!*'

Séamus an chaca – James the shit – is the 'honorary' title bestowed on James for his precipitous retreat from the battle and his general negative view of the Irish people. Peter Berresford Ellis's account of the battle in *The Boyne Water* (1989) says:

> The Williamites celebrated by striking a medal which portrayed James running away after the Boyne and, on the reverse side, was a deer with winged hooves and the Latin inscription '*pedibus timor addidit alas* [fear added wings to his feet]'.

The Irish would have agreed with that image.

> After the Battle of the Boyne, King James was fleeing to Dublin, and he fell as he was crossing over a gate. That is how King's Gate got its name, though the exact location of the gate is not known. As he was passing Tara an old woman shouted to him, 'Your Majesty won the race.'
>
> (Joseph Wall, aged 43, Kings Gate, Duleek, collector Ronan Brennan, 1938, NFCS 0682:267-8)

Ellis states:

> Williamite propaganda afterwards had it that James had made his headquarters in the ruined church at Donore, and, indeed, had remained there out of harm's way until he saw the fording of the river at Oldbridge. This was, of course, quite untrue.

But local tradition has it otherwise. Patrick McGuinness, 50, of Oldbridge told the Schools Collection in 1938:

> It is said that King James watched the Battle of the Boyne from Donore Churchyard. When he saw that his men were being beaten, he fled through Donore on his way to Dublin. The people in Donore asked him how the battle was going on, and he said, 'It is all done over.' It is believed locally that that is how Donore came to be called 'Donover'. It is still called 'Donover' by the older people, and some of the carts have 'Donover' on them.
>
> (Collected by Patrick's daughter, Peggie, NFCS 0682:5)

The truth seems to be somewhere in the middle. George Story reported:

> King James, during part of the Action at the Boyn, stood at the little old Church upon the Hill called Dunore, but when he saw how things were like to go, he marched off to Duleek, and from thence towards Dublin ...

7

THE WHITE HORSE
OF THE PEPPERS

Ballygarth Castle on the River Nanny in Julianstown was owned by the Pepper family from 1660 until Gerald Pepper lost the property as a result of supporting King James. After the Battle of the Boyne in 1690 his land was given in lieu of wages to a Williamite cavalry officer, who set off immediately from Dublin to find and claim his new possession. As a stranger in the country, he was forced to rely on local people for directions, and as one of the conquerors, he was led dangerously astray in a particularly vicious form of the Irish pastime of 'send the fool farther.'

Samuel Lover's version of the family legend in *Legends and Stories of Ireland* (1831, 1834) takes full advantage of the potential for burlesque. A shoe on the soldier's horse has come off 5 miles from the nearest blacksmith, because his self-appointed guide from Dublin to Ballygarth, Gerald Pepper's foster brother Rory, had loosened it.

'Confound it!' said the soldier. 'Five miles, and this barbarous road, and your long miles into the bargain.' (The Irish mile in the seventeenth century was 1.27 English miles.)

'Sure, I don't deny the road is not the best,' said Rory, 'but if it's not good, sure we give you good measure at all events.'

Nightfall overtook them at Duleek, where the nearest smithy – according to Rory – was located, but Rory quickly brought the blacksmith into the plot so that he couldn't be found.

Then Rory turned the Englishman over to the tender care of the young son of his cousin, who duly guided the man, with his lame horse, through twisting byways, until he led him into a swamp and absconded. It was dark by the time the trooper eventually extricated himself and his horse, and he wandered the roads until he saw a light. As luck would have it, he had fetched up at Ballygarth Castle.

Gerald Pepper was at home, and he welcomed the exhausted traveller with the usual Irish hospitality, although Rory had returned and reported on his doings with the trooper, and Pepper had a good idea who his visitor was. The Englishman insisted on seeing his disabled horse to the stable before sitting down to supper, and on examining the shoeless hoof knew that he would not be able to ride it the following day. As he left the stable he noticed the magnificent white charger that had carried Pepper into battle with such gallantry that King James himself had nicknamed Pepper 'the White Horseman'.

During the meal, the trooper asked Pepper if he knew anyone in the neighbourhood called Gerald Pepper. Pepper said that there was a person of that name.

'Is his property a good one?' said the trooper, in Lover's version of the story.

'Very much reduced of late,' replied Gerald.

'Ballygarth they call it,' said the soldier. 'Is that far from here?'

'It would puzzle me to tell you how to get to it from this place,' was the answer.

'It is very provoking,' said the trooper. 'I have been looking for it these three days, and cannot find it, and nobody seems to know where it is.'

He explained that he had come to take possession of the forfeited Ballygarth, but since most people seemed not to have heard of it he reckoned that it must not be worth much. Besides, he was on a four-day leave and had to return to Dublin the following day, which would not be possible with his own lame horse. So he proposed a bargain: since he needed a horse, and he wasn't sure if he would ever return to the vicinity to occupy the property, he offered to give Gerald Pepper the debenture from King William entitling the holder to Ballygarth, in exchange for the white charger he had seen in the stable.

Much as Pepper hated to part with his prized possession, it was the only way to save his property, and so he agreed.

Lover ends the story thus:

> Gerald Pepper looked after his noble steed while he remained within sight, and thought no one was witness to the tear he dashed from his eye when he turned to re-enter his house … To perpetuate to his descendant the remembrance of the singular event which had preserved to him his estate, the white horse was introduced into his armorial bearings, and is, at this day, one of the heraldic distinctions of the family.

A local account says that the horse managed to throw the trooper off on his way to Dublin and returned to Ballygarth.

All Thoroughbreds trace their ancestry to three stallions: the Godolphin Barb, the Darley Arabian and the Byerley Turk. The career of the Byerley Turk (1680–1706) closely resembles that of the White Horse of the Peppers. His name was Azarax. He served as a charger in many battles and was captured as spoils of war but proved unmanageable by the man who got him. He came into the ownership of Captain Robert Byerley, who brought him to Ireland. The horse won a race at Downpatrick on his way to the Battle of the Boyne, where he fought with distinction on the Williamite side under Captain Byerley.

Most Thoroughbreds come from the Darley Arabian; only 5 per cent come from the Byerley Turk. One of his twenty-first-generation descendants is the 2013 wonder horse Sprinter Sacre, who won his tenth chase in a row – fourteen of sixteen races in all – at Punchestown on 23 April on his first visit to Ireland. Search the internet and compare the contemporary painting of the Byerley Turk by John Wooton (c. 1682–1764) with a photograph of Sprinter Sacre: dark brown, large body, relatively small head. Pity he's a gelding.

8

THREEFOLD
DEATHS

Triple or threefold death, in which a person is killed by three methods, has mythic, mystical, legendary and historical resonances. A story about Merlin is one example.

He caught his sister *in flagrante* with a man who was not her husband and hinted that he might reveal her secret. In order to destroy his credibility in advance, she asked him to foretell how a boy would die, and he answered that he would fall from a rock. She disguised the boy as a girl and asked how she would die. Merlin said she would come to a violent death in a tree. She disguised the boy as another boy and asked again. Merlin said he would drown. Merlin was ridiculed for seemingly being a fool, but when the boy grew to manhood, he fell from his horse when it slipped on a high rock, his foot got stuck in a tree overhanging a river, and his head was submerged so that he drowned.

Lindow Man, the Iron Age bog body discovered in England in 1984, was strangled and hit on the head, and his throat was cut, in what is described as a ritual killing. Eamonn P. Kelly, bog-body specialist at the National Museum of Ireland, reckons that many of the bog bodies found here were nobles ritually killed and buried deliberately on political borders and in between-world earth-water bogs as a propitiation to the earth goddess. He draws a parallel between those bodies and the threefold ritual-like deaths of kings of legendary history, such as those related in the stories below.

A curious survival of a ritual boundary burial could be seen in funeral ceremonies recalled by 69-year-old Daniel Lynch of Leitrim, Mullagh, Moynalty in 1942 (collector P.J. Gaynor, NFC 830:7): they would set the corpse down three times; first, when they were leaving the yard of the house, second, on leaving the dead person's land, and third, on leaving the townland.

A modern threefold death is that of the controversial Russian 'Mad Monk' Rasputin, who was poisoned, shot (three times) and drowned in 1916 after surviving a near-fatal stabbing two years earlier, according to substantially reliable reports.

Some people, like Rasputin, are simply very hard to kill, but in the case of a king – a ruler by divine right – magic or supernatural intervention is deemed necessary. As the seventeenth-century Irish historian Geoffrey Keating pointed out: 'It was by God who is Lord and ruler over all, that he has been appointed king over the peoples to govern them.' Also, those who plan to assassinate a king would want to be very sure he is dead, since the consequences of a failed attempt at such a serious crime would be fatal.

Commentators point out that these stories reflect a power struggle between Church and State, not only in the early Middle Ages, when they are set, but also in the eleventh century, when the stories were probably written. Joan Radner (1983) has said that wounding, burning and drowning is 'the characteristically Irish form of the threefold death,' which is 'an explicitly Christian narrative device' to demonstrate 'that God will punish and purge significant wrongdoing.'

Irish legendary history records three dramatic threefold deaths of kings: Laeghaire son of Niall of the Nine Hostages, Muirchertach mac Ercae, and Diarmait mac Cerbaill. (Calling these stories 'legendary' does not imply that they have no basis in fact.)

LAEGHAIRE

Laeghaire, high king 428–462, invaded Leinster to impose the ongoing Cattle Tribute, lost the battle, and was allowed to return home with his head still on his shoulders on condition that he swear a sacred oath by the elements – earth, air and fire – that he would never again attempt to take cattle from Leinster. Two years later, he violated the vow and took cattle, so he was cursed: 'Earth to swallow him, Sun to scorch him, Wind (his breath) to pass away from him.' The curse was fulfilled when he was struck by lightning, stopped breathing and was buried at Rath Laeghaire on the Hill of Tara, standing and facing Leinster in eternal defiance.

> The elements of God, which he had pledged as guarantee,
> Inflicted the doom of death on the king.
>
> (*Chronicum Scotorum*)

MUIRCHERTACH MAC ERCAE

Muirchertach mac Ercae, who reigned 507–536, was an uncle of St Colmcille. He is also known as Muirchertach mac Muiredaig for his father or simply Mac Ercae after his mother, Erca, who left her husband, Sarran, who was king of Britain, and eloped to Ireland with Muiredaig. Sarran then married Erca's sister, Babona. Babona's sons included Cairnech and Luirig. Cairnech built a monastery. Sarran died and Luirig succeeded to the throne and started to build a fort within the precinct of Cairnech's monastery.

At the time, Muirchertach was in Britain, learning military science. He had been expelled from Ireland for a killing, had gone to Scotland, and was expelled from there for killing Loarn, king of Scotland, who was his mother's father. Muirchertach was with his cousin Cairnech, having his weapons consecrated by him, when Luirig started building his fort, and Cairnech told Muirchertach, 'You will be king of Britain and Ireland forever, and after that you will go to Heaven, if you prevent Luirig from using his power against the church.'

Muirchertach went to Luirig and told him that Cairnech wanted him to stop building the fort.

'As God is my judge,' said Luirig, 'I think more of the power of Cairnech's pet fawn than of his power or the power of the Lord God who he adores.'

Muirchertach reported Luirig's response to Cairnech, who became very angry and said, 'I pray to God that the fawn will be the cause of his death, and by your hand, Mac Ercae.' He told Muirchertach to go and destroy Luirig. Then God performed a miracle. He sent the fawn to Luirig's people, and they all began to chase it, except Luirig and his women. Muirchertach went to Luirig and speared him and brought his head back to Cairnech. He later married Luirig's widow and together with Cairnech became king of Britain for seven years, and when the Franks and Saxons attacked he defeated them.

He then came to Ireland with a large fleet and landed at Fan-na-long on the Boyne near Drogheda and burned his ships. He killed the provincial kings and 'took their sovereignty by right for ever, for himself and for his descendants,' according to the Irish Nennius, the source of the above account.

Cairnech founded an abbey at Dulane, north of Kells, in the sixth century and is the patron saint of the town. Niall of the Nine Hostages, who died in the previous century, was the first person buried there. Cairnech disinterred his body, said a Mass over it, and reburied it at Dulane. But there are two St Cairnechs. Historians are unsure which did what, and some say there was really only one Cairnech. One has a feast day of 28 March and the other 16 May.

Cairnech the Just helped St Patrick compile the Senchas Már, a conflation of Irish native pagan and Christian law done mainly in Nobber over three years beginning in 438, and he is credited as one of the 'Nine Pillars' of the Senchas Már. The *Dictionary of National Biography* gives the death date of Muirchertach's cousin Cairnech as 539. There is an easy way out of this dilemma without giving one man a lifespan of well over 100 years. Although some commentators assume that Cairnech the Just was a contemporary of Patrick, he didn't need to be. The Senchas Már, a compendium of precedent and case law rather than legislated statutes, was amended, modified and updated many times over the years by a number of brehons (Irish judges) and jurists, and one of those could have been Muirchertach's cousin, who came to Ireland with him.

Muirchertach's threefold death by poison, fire and water came about through the magic and machinations of a woman who identified herself by several names. One of those names is Sín (pronounced 'sheen'), which means 'Storm', and that is the name she is called by in the story. She claimed to be human, but her actions seem like those of a Sídh (Sidhe) or fairy woman of the Otherworld. In some tellings of the story she is called a witch or a banshee.

The *Annals of Tigernach* report for AD 534 (*recte* 536):

The death of Muirchertach mac Ercae in a vat of wine on Samhain Eve [31 October] at the hill of Cletech over the Boyne. As Cairnech said:

> I greatly fear the woman
> round whom many storms will move,
> for the man who fire will burn
> and wine will drown at Cletech.

> Storm of many magic names –
> She has killed you, Mac Ercae.

The story is fleshed out dramatically in 'The Violent Death of Muirchertach mac Ercae', an eleventh-century story mainly from the fourteenth-fifteenth-century *Yellow Book of Lecan*.

Muirchertach was living in the House of Cletech overlooking the Boyne at the present Rosnaree, across the river from Brú na Bóinne (Newgrange). He was hunting one day next to the Brú, and his companions left him alone on his hunting mound. He was not long there when he saw a young woman sitting near him on the mound. She was fine-formed and fair-haired with lustrous skin, wearing a green cloak. He had never seen such a beautiful and noble woman, and his body and spirit were so filled with love that he felt he would give all of Ireland for one night with her. He greeted her like an old friend.

'What's the story?'

'I'll tell you,' she replied. 'I'm in love with Muirchertach mac Ercae, and I've come here to find him.'

That sounded good to Muirchertach, and he said, 'Do you recognise me, young lady?'

'I do,' she said. 'I am knowledgeable about other places and other company, and I recognise you and the rest of the men of Ireland.'

'Will you come with me?'

'I will, if you give me what I want.'

'I'll give you power over me.'

'Do I have your word for that?'

'You have,' he said, and then she sang:

> Not untimely is that power,
>   but if clerics have their say,
> nothing tender will be ours,
>   not for even one full day.

> What the clergymen have taught
>   on women – don't believe it.
> Clergymen will give you naught:
>   nothing for your benefit.

And Muirchertach replied:

> Don't rebuke the clergymen,
>   brilliant woman, sweet of speech,
> when it's best that everyone
>   follows what the clergy teach.

> Woman, don't say such a thing.
>   Don't abuse the holy men.
> They are loyal to the king.
>   Never would they injure him.

Then he said, 'I will give you 100 cattle from each of my herds, 100 cups, 100 gold mantles, and a feast every second night in the House of Cletech.'

'Ah, no,' she said. 'None of those adornments. This is what I want: that you never speak my name, that I never come face to face with your wife, Duaibsech, and that the clergy never come into the house that I am in.'

'I give you that because I have promised, though I'd rather give you half of Ireland instead. Now, tell me, what is your name, so I can avoid speaking it?'

'Sigh, Melody, Storm, Rough Wind, Wintry, Groan, Lamentation. Those are my names.'

True to his word, Muirchertach evicted his wife and children and all his Uí Néill relatives – two battalions of them. Duaibsech went to Cairnech at Dulane to complain to him.

'O, cleric, bless my body. I'm afraid of death tonight. A woman of the Sídh has come to our house, and she treated me with contempt.'

Cairnech went to Cletech, but Storm refused to let him in. This made Cairnech angry, and he dug a symbolic grave in front of the house and laid a curse on Muirchertach: 'The man for whom I made this grave is finished. It is truly the end of his reign.'

As a blessing for the rest of the Uí Néill clan he gave them three powerful relics to ensure victory in battle: the Cathach (Battler) of Colmcille – the psalter that Colmcille was believed to have written – the Bell of St Patrick, and his own Mísach, apparently a martyrology.

When Cairnech returned to his monastery at Dulane, he met a delegation of Munstermen who wished to make a treaty with Muirchertach. He went with them to Cletech, and when Muirchertach learned of their mission he came out of the house. But he saw Cairnech and said, 'Why have you come here, cleric, after cursing me?'

Cairnech explained that he wanted to make peace between the two clans, so Muirchertach held his objections. Cairnech took blood from Muirchertach and the Munster leader, Tadg, and mixed it in a vessel and declared the treaty done. Then Muirchertach told Cairnech to leave.

Back in the house, Muirchertach decided that he wanted to know more about Storm, and he said, 'Tell me, clever lady, do you believe in the God of the clerics, and where do you come from, and who are your people?'

'I am the daughter of a man and a woman of the seed of Eve and Adam, and so I am worthy of you. I believe in the same true God as the clerics, but there is no miracle they could work that I can't match. I could create a sun and a moon and bright shining stars, fighting men, wine from Boyne water, sheep from stones, pigs from bracken, gold and silver.'

'Let's see you work some of these great miracles,' said Muirchertach.

Storm went out and produced two great battalions, equal in strength and ability, and Muirchertach and his people watched them for a while as they wounded and slaughtered one another. Then he called for water to be drawn from the Boyne and brought into the house, and he asked Storm to change it into wine. She did so, and when the people tried it they said they had never tasted better. Then she turned bracken into pigs and served the meat and wine to the company, and when they had eaten the enchanted food they believed they had been well fed.

However, in the morning they all felt weak and wasted, but they went outside, and Muirchertach said to Storm, 'Show us more of your skills.'

She changed stones into four battalions of fighting men on the green in front of Brú na Bóinne, and Muirchertach took up his weapons and charged in among them. But every man he killed rose up immediately against him, and at the end of the day he was exhausted. Storm fed him and his companions the same food and drink. When they awoke in the morning they had neither strength nor energy.

'I am without strength, lovely lady,' he said to Storm. 'My head is confused, my right hand is useless, my defences are down.'

But there came a shout of challenge from the Brú, and Muirchertach went out and saw two great battalions, one of blue men and the other of headless men. He charged into them, wounding and killing, until Storm came and gave him kingship over them. But when he went to return to Cletech, there were two huge battalions between him and the house, so he charged them and began to fight.

Cairnech knew what was happening, and he sent Masan, Casan and Cridan to help the king. When they arrived, they saw him hacking at stones and sods and stalks, and they told him that he was under a spell and advised him to make the sign of the cross over his face. He did so and saw that there was nothing but stones and sods in front of him. He asked them why they had come, and they answered, 'For your body, because death is near to you.'

They marked the outline of a church and told him to dig a trench for it in honour of God, which he did. That was the first damage ever done to the green in front of the Brú. He thanked the Son of God that his madness was ended, and he made a rather boasting confession to the clerics, in which he summarised his career of battles and killings. Then he repented of his sins, and the clerics gave him holy water and Communion. They made camp in the outline of the church.

He returned to Cletech and sat next to Storm. She asked him why he had stopped fighting, and he told her the clerics had come and blessed him, and then he didn't see anything but bracken and stones and puff-balls and twigs. Storm repeated her warnings about the clerics and told him he was better off with her. Enthralled yet again, Muirchertach said:

> I will never part from thee,
> maiden fine of form and sweet.
> Dearer is your face to me
> than the churches of the priests.

Storm made more magic wine for them that night, and when they were all intoxicated there came the sound of a great wind outside.

'That is the sigh of a wintry night,' said Muirchertach, speaking two of the woman's names. Then Storm created a snow storm that sounded like a raging battle. He went outside and returned.

'It's a bad night tonight,' he said. 'There has never been one so bad. I've never seen a night the likes of this one.'

They all lay down at the end of the feast, and not one of them had the strength of a woman in childbirth. Muirchertach fell into a deep sleep, but he woke up with a scream.

'What's the matter?' asked Storm.

'I saw a great phantom,' he said, 'and red flames and the House of Cletech on fire and an everlasting flame on my head by a magic spell.'

He went outside and saw a fire in the outlined little church by the Brú where the clerics were camping. He went to them and told them of his vision and said, 'I have no strength or energy tonight, and I wouldn't be able to defend myself if I was attacked because of the weakness and the bad night that's in it.' The clerics spoke to him, and he returned to Cletech and Storm.

'It's very bad for the clerics tonight in their camp,' he told her, 'because of the severity of the storm.'

'Why did you speak my name, man?' she said. 'Your end has come. Your strength is finished.'

'That's true. My death is near, for there was a prophecy that my death and the death of my grandfather Loarn would be similar. It was not in battle he died but by burning alive.'

'Go to sleep, then, and I will watch over you. If it is your fate, the house will not be burned over you tonight.'

'I'm afraid Tuathal Máelgarb might come and attack the house.' (Tuathal, Muirchertach's cousin, became the next high king.)

'If he does come, it won't be tonight. Go to sleep now.'

He asked her for a drink, and she put a sleep spell on the wine to make him drunk and feeble. He fell into a deep sleep and saw in a vision that he went onto a ship on the sea, and the ship sank, and a griffin snatched him in her talons and took him to her nest, and the nest went on fire with him in it, and then he and the griffin fell.

Muirchertach got up and went to his foster brother Dub dá Rind, the son of a druid, and asked him to interpret the vision.

'The ship is your kingdom on the sea of life,' he said, 'and you are steering the kingdom. The sinking of the ship means your life is coming to an end. The griffin that took you to her nest is the woman who has made you drunk and taken you into her bed to keep you in the House of Cletech so that it will burn over you. And the griffin that fell with you is the woman who will die because of you.'

Storm then cast a sleep spell on Muirchertach, and she took all the spears and javelins of the company in the house and arranged them at the doors so that they pointed toward the house. She went out and magicked up a crowd of people all around the house. She came back in and set fires in every corner of the house and on the walls, and then got into bed.

Muirchertach suddenly woke up.

'What is it?' she said.

'I saw a host of phantoms burning the house over me and slaughtering my people at the door.'

'There's no harm to you from that. It's only your imagination.'

As they were speaking they could hear the sound of the fire and the cries of the demon host and the magic around the house.

'Who is surrounding the house?' asked the king.

'It is Tuathal Máelgarb with his army,' said Storm. 'He has come to avenge the battle of Granard on you.'

Muirchertach did not know that this was a lie and that there were no humans surrounding the house. He got out of bed and went to find his weapons, but found no one to help him. Storm went outside, and he tried to follow her, but everything between him and the door was on fire. He went into the dining hall and got into the vat of wine that was there. Then the roof fell on his head, and the fire burned 5ft of the length of his body – all but the parts that were immersed in the wine.

Cairnech and the clerics took Muirchertach's body to Dulane for burial. When Duaibsech, Muirchertach's wife, met them there, she died of grief, and they were buried together on the north side of the church.

They saw a beautiful mournful woman coming toward them wearing a silk smock and a green cloak with gold fringe. They recognised her as the one who had enchanted the king, and they asked her who she was and what she had against him that she should destroy him.

'My name is Storm,' she said, 'daughter of Sighi son of Déin son of Truin. Muirchertach killed my mother and father and brother and sister in the Battle of Cerb on the Boyne [Assey, near Bective], and he destroyed the Old Tribes of Tara and all my ancestors in that battle.'

She confessed that she had poisoned Muirchertach and expressed sorrow for her deeds and said that she would die of grief, which she immediately did. Cairnech ordered that she be buried across the foot of Muirchertach's and Duaibsech's graves. He prayed for Muirchertach's soul but did not bring it out of Hell.

DIARMAIT MAC CERBAILL

Tuathal Máelgarb (536–544) succeeded Muirchertach mac Ercae as king, and Diarmait mac (Fergus) Cerbaill (544–565) succeeded Tuathal. They were all great-grandsons of Niall of the Nine Hostages.

'*Máell maol*' describes a person whose hair is close-cropped, like Granuaile (Gráinne Mhaol). In the case of a cleric it refers to the tonsure. As part of a person's name it indicates devotion to a saint, like Maolodrán. But Tuathal's sobriquet, 'Rough-cropped' or 'Bald-rough', had a peculiar origin. Geoffrey Keating explains that when his mother gave birth to him 'she struck his head against a stone as a ceremony foreboding success for him, and the stone made a hollow in his head, and no hair grew in that hollow.' *Cóir Anmann* (Fitness of Names) adds that he was 'so called because his head was bald and lumpy.' *Maelgarb* is also the name of a fatal cattle disease (eDIL).

When Tuathal was king, he saw Diarmait as a threat to his throne – with good reason – and outlawed him and put a price on his head. He promised a reward to anyone who would bring him Diarmait's heart. Diarmait was in hiding in the wetlands of the Shannon when he happened to arrive at Snámh dá Én (Two Birds Swimming) just as St Ciarán was beginning to build Clonmacnoise.

'Thrust in the upright with me,' Ciarán said to Diarmait, 'with my hand over yours, so that you will become king of Ireland.'

'But how can that happen?' said Diarmait. 'Tuathal is king.'

'That is a matter for God,' Ciarán replied.

Diarmait did as Ciarán ordered – that scene is depicted on the tenth-century Cross of the Scriptures at Clonmacnoise – and Ciarán told him that he would become high king next day.

When Diarmait's foster brother, Maol Mór, heard that, he offered to kill Tuathal for him, and asked Diarmait for the loan of his prized black horse to accomplish the task. Diarmait dithered, worried that he might lose his valuable steed if the mission failed, but eventually gave in.

Maol Mór acquired the heart of a dog, skewered it on the head of a spear, and sped frantically on the black horse to where Tuathal was staying that night at Grellach Eilte, west of Crossakeel. He announced excitedly that he had Diarmait's heart to give to Tuathal, and because of his urgency he was allowed to approach the king. He did so at full gallop and never stopped until he had pierced Tuathal's heart with the spear. If he thought he could get away with such a spectacular assassination he was mistaken. He was immediately seized by Tuathal's

friends and killed, whence comes the saying 'the valorous deed of Maol Mór' to describe a Pyrrhic victory.

Diarmait thus became king and was inaugurated a few days later. He invited Ciarán to the ceremony and went to meet him at Cnoc Brecáin, between Uisneach and Clonmacnoise.

'You helped me become king,' Diarmait said, 'so I want to give you this territory, together with the oxen and cows, for your church.'

This seems to be roughly an area stretching from Ballymore, which is midway between Mullingar and Athlone, to Clonmacnoise. The land had belonged to Flann, son of Dima, an enemy of Diarmait. Sometime previously, Diarmait had found himself in the vicinity and took the opportunity to kill Flann. He wounded Flann, who took refuge in his house. Diarmait set the house on fire, and Flann went into a tub of water to escape the flames and died there. Knowing how Diarmait had obtained the property, Ciarán angrily refused the gift.

'I will accept nothing from you or your sons,' he said, 'and furthermore, the same death you gave to Flann will be your own death: to be wounded, drowned and burnt.'

If that wasn't enough warning, many years later he received another prophecy. He had killed Suibne and taken Suibne's young son, Black Áedh, into his house. Beg mac Dé, who was the best seer in his time, was attached to Diarmait's court. In front of Diarmait and Black Áedh, Beg said that Diarmait would be poisoned by Black Áedh in the house of Banbán the innkeeper, while he was wearing a shirt woven from a single flax seed and a mantle woven from a single sheep, drinking ale brewed from a single grain of corn, with bacon on his plate from a pig that was never born; and the ridge beam of Diarmait's own house would fall on his head. (St Ruadán, who cursed Tara, also made the ridge beam prophecy.)

Diarmait exiled Black Áedh and had the ridge beam removed and thrown into the Irish Sea. Later, after Beg mac Dé's death (557), he asked his magicians for a second opinion, and they confirmed Beg's prediction.

'All this is unlikely,' said Diarmait.

Years afterwards, Diarmait was invited to dine in the house of Banbán in Rathbeg, County Antrim. His host clothed and fed him, and the way he described the origins of the food and ale and clothing accorded with the prophecies. Looking up, Diarmait commented that most of the house was new, but the roof beam seemed older.

'Yes,' said Banbán. 'One day we were fishing in our currachs on the Irish Sea, and we saw a roof beam floating toward us, so as a curiosity I took it and built this house around it.'

Suddenly realising that all the prophecies had now fallen into place, Diarmait made a rush for the door, but Black Áedh was there before him and thrust a spear into him so that it broke his spine, and then set the house on fire. Diarmait managed to get back inside and crawled into the ale vat. Then the roof beam fell and killed him.

According to Adomnán, Colmcille cursed Black Áedh to die by a spear thrust, by falling from wood and by drowning, because of his killing of Diarmait. He was wounded by a spear, fell from the spar of a ship and drowned.

9

CORMAC
MAC AIRT

Cormac and BrianBorú are the two most famous high kings, but while Brian, who reigned 1002–1014, is firmly established historically, Cormac's life is enveloped in the mists of legend, and folklorists tend to classify him as mythical. Medieval historians, however, who embraced history and legend equally, say he was king from 227 to 266.

His mother's father, a druid, put five protections on him: against wounding, fire, drowning, sorcery and wolves. A pack of wolves snatched him while his mother was asleep and adopted him briefly, until he was found and returned to her.

Probably the best-known story about him is the objection he made to the judgment of Lugaid, who took the kingship after Cormac's father was killed. A man asked Lugaid to order a woman whose sheep had grazed on his land to give him the sheep in compensation. Lugaid agreed, but young Cormac said fair compensation would be one shearing for another: the woman should give the man one year's shearing of the sheep to pay for the shearing of the grass. The people agreed; Lugaid was forced out of the kingship and Cormac installed.

THE FIRST WATER MILL IN IRELAND

Irish raiders captured a Scottish princess named Ciarnait and brought her back to Ireland. Some say she was the most beautiful woman in the land. When Cormac saw her he took her as his mistress. However, his wife, Eithne the Slender, who was also said to be the most beautiful woman in Ireland (see chapter 11), took a firm stand and removed Ciarnait from Cormac and put her in charge of grinding grain.

She would have been using a rotary hand quern, a relatively recent Iron Age innovation in these islands and one that was widely used well into historical times. It was a vast improvement on the Stone Age saddle quern, but still labour intensive. Ciarnait was a conscientious worker, filling ten bushels every day, which was enough to feed hundreds of people.

One day, Cormac came to her while she was in her house working alone and seduced her. After a few months, heavy with child, she was no longer able to do the grinding.

Being a righteous king, Cormac took pity on her and imported a millwright from Scotland to build a water mill, the first in Ireland, on the River Gabhra, which runs through the Gabhra Valley between the Hill of Tara and the Hill of Skryne. The river is fed by a stream called Nith, which flows from the well of Nemnach at the 'elf-mound' on the northeast part of the Hill of Tara.

The mill was sited at Lismullin (the Enclosure of the Mill) on the north side of the N3, where Opus Dei now operates a conference and retreat centre opposite the lane leading up to Tara. This would have been a horizontal mill, powered by a horizontal wheel beneath the mill housing. The earliest of these in Ireland have been dated by archaeologists to the seventh century. A convent with a mill was founded there in 1242, and that could be the reason for the name Lismullin.

DEATH OF CORMAC

One of Cormac's sons, Ceallach, took prisoner a man under the protection of Aonghus Gaoibuaibhtheach (of the Mighty Spear), whose weapon of choice was a spear with three chains attached. Aonghus came to Tara to confront Ceallach, who was standing behind Cormac, and cast the spear at him and killed him. But a chain hit the king in the face, blinding him in one eye. A king had to be physically perfect, and the half-blind Cormac was forced to relinquish the throne to his son Cairbre, and he retired to Achall (Hill of Skryne).

Two years later, he was living at Cletech (Rosnaree) – and some say it was he who built it – where he died under mysterious circumstances. He was eating a piece of bread when a fishbone stuck in his throat and choked him. The debate has never been settled: whether the bone was accidentally mixed in with the bread dough, or the druids inserted it, or the druids somehow magicked the bone into his throat.

'On account of the excellence of Cormac's deeds and judgments, and laws, God gave him the light of the Faith seven years before his death,' according to Geoffrey Keating. The druids and the people were worshipping a golden calf, and the druids asked Cormac why he didn't worship it as well. Cormac replied that he would sooner worship the craftsman who made the calf than the calf itself. 'I worship only the one true God of Heaven.'

Keating reports:

> After this his food was cooked for the king, and he began to eat a
> portion of a salmon from the Boyne. Thereupon the demon sprites
> came, at the instigation of Maoilgheann the druid, and they killed
> the king. Others say that it was a salmon-bone that stuck in his
> throat and choked him. For it was eating fish he was when the
> sprites, or demons of the air, choked him.

Cormac had told his people that he did not wish to be buried at Brú
na Bóinne (Newgrange) where the pagan kings of the past had been
laid to rest. When his followers tried to take his body across the Boyne
to the Brú anyway, the water rose against them three times, and the
body was torn from the bier and deposited at Rosnaree – the Wooded
Hill of the King – for which it is named.

St Colmcille came later to Rosnaree and said thirty Masses for
Cormac, who is reckoned to have been one of the first three Christians
in Ireland, along with his father, Art, and King Conor of Ulster.

10

ARDBRACCAN
AND ST ULTÁN

In the fourth century BC, King Conaing Begeglach was holding an assembly at Tara, when they saw a huge man coming toward them from the west carrying a branch bearing apples, nuts, acorns, and berries. This was Fintan, the sole survivor of the Great Deluge in Ireland, who was reincarnated many times over the centuries in human and animal form. He shook the branch, scattering the seeds, which were taken by people and planted all around the country. From these seeds grew the five ancient sacred trees of Ireland, which were all blown down in the seventh century.

The ash Bile Tortan grew in the Plain of Tortan at Ardbraccan near Navan; the wood of the fallen yew Eo Rossa in Carlow was used for shingles on the monastery of Durrow; the oak Craebh Mughna stood in Kildare; the ash Craebh Dathi was in Farbill, County Westmeath; and the ash Bile Uisnigh stood on the Hill of Uisneach in Westmeath. A sacred tree is called *bile* in Irish, and that element is still retained in some of the place-names where such trees were honoured, such as Farbill, Rathvily in Carlow and Billywood near Moynalty in Meath, and many others that are not included in the shortlist of the five most important.

In 433, St Patrick founded a church next to Bile Tortan at Ardbraccan, where his nephew St Breacain established a monastery in the early seventh century. Patrick was following the same course of action recommended for missionaries to the English by Pope Gregory the Great in the following century: don't destroy the places of pagan worship, but convert them to Christian churches so that the people 'may abandon the error in their hearts and know and adore the true God, while still resorting familiarly to the places to which they are accustomed.'

When Bile Tortan was blown down in a storm about the year 600, a number of holy men and poets composed a lament. One of these was St Ultán mac hUa Conchobair (d. 657), bishop at Ardbraccan and author of the biography of St Brigit from which all other accounts of her life probably derive. He was related to Brigit on her mother's side. Some say he was Brigit's uncle or nephew, but since she died in 525 that seems unlikely. However, according to the *Annals of the Four Masters*, he was 180 years old when he died. Fortuitously, as if to support that claim, the obit for St Mochaemhog, who died the preceding year, avers: 'Thirteen years and four hundred was the length of his life.'

Ultán also wrote a Life of St Patrick and composed hymns in Brigit's honour, and he wrote the lament on King Blathmac's sons killed by the Leinster champion Maelodrán (see chapter 1):

> Red meal the millstones grind.
> A king's sons supplied the grist
> for the mill of Maelodrán.

This is a condensed version of the curiously pagan-sounding epitaph that Ultán and seven others, including Colmcille, made for the great Bile Tortan: some 80ft (25m) in diameter and 500ft (150m) high. Each man took one line at a time with most contributing several:

> Fallen is the Tree of Tortu, whose skirts conquered many a storm. Sad are all the men of Tortu, mourning for that single tree; dearer to them is the thing they see than all things that are gone from us. When the men of Tortu used to meet together round the huge conspicuous tree, the pelting of the storms did not reach them, until the day when it was decayed.
>
> Though it is withered now, it had not an early end: long has it been on earth: the King who created its form has brought it low again.

Fifty cubits is the thickness of the tree that overpeered the array of the forest: three hundred cubits, famous count was the full height of its timber.

It found an abode over strong Tortu from the time of the sons of mighty Míl, until its colour faded and it fell, in the time of the sons of Aed Slane. [The 'sons of mighty Míl' – the Milesians – came to Ireland about 1500 BC, which would make Bile Tortan some 2,000 years old when it died.]

A wind laid the Tree low – none that is not hard of heart can bear the loss – and it crushed thrice fifty victims of the Conaille, at their fair. [That line was composed by Croin. Another poet took issue with his sentiments.]

I am Mochua: I bid Croin not to grieve excessively: from the roots of the illustrious Tree many a tree might spring.

No comfort have I, though the winds stir the treetops of the wood to laughter: to-day a solitary housewife breaks firewood from the Tree of Tortu.

Though the wind made rough sport with it, it could not break the Tree while it was young; but it brings to the ground all that is old: this I know by the Tree of Tortu.

The 'Conaille' mentioned above was the Buidhe Connail – the Yellow Plague – which devastated Britain and Ireland in the 540s and again in 664–666. Medical historians believe it was a complication of jaundice resulting from the bubonic plague. The latter outbreak in Ireland is said to have come about through political and religious meddling. The joint high kings, Blathmac and Diarmaid, the sons of Áed Sláine, were troubled about the overpopulation of Ireland, and they asked the holy men to pray to God to bring a great pestilence to kill the poor people. All prayers are answered, and God granted their wish – in His own way. The high kings and those holy men who acceded to the kings' request to storm Heaven were among those who died. Francis J. Byrne (*Irish Kings and High Kings*) said that the plague 'brought an end not only to the golden age of saints but also to the generations of kings mighty enough to become heroes of saga.'

Although Ultán's death date is usually given as 656 or 657, he is said to have survived the plague, which is probably why some records say he died in the 660s.

He loved children – he had 500 foster children and is now designated the patron saint of paediatricians – and he was kept busy providing for the orphans of the victims of the plague. During this time a large fleet approached the coast intent on invasion, and King Diarmaid asked Ultán to do something. Ultán was occupied feeding the children with his right hand, but he raised his left hand against the fleet and 'wrecked, destroyed, stranded thrice fifty ships,' whence comes the proverb, 'Ultán's left hand against evil,' according to the *Martyrology of Oengus*. He told Diarmaid that if his right hand had been free, not only would he have repelled that invasion, but Ireland would never again be invaded forever.

There is a St Ultán's special school in Navan and a national school in Dublin, and the first dedicated infants' hospital in Dublin was St Ultán's, founded in 1919 by Kathleen Lynn, a unit commander in the Citizens' Army in 1916. The *Book of Saint Ultan*, featuring contributions by Jack Yeats, Harry Clarke, Æ, and other luminaries of the time, was published in 1920 to help support the hospital. It closed in 1984, when it was amalgamated with the National Children's Hospital.

Ultán's feast day is 4 September.

11

KELLS

Dún Chúile Sibhrinne was founded as a fortified royal residence by Fiacha Finnailches, king of Ireland, about 1200 BC, according to the *Annals of the Four Masters*. It was later called Ceann Lios – Head Palace – Cenandas, Cenannus na Ríg, Ceanannus, expanded to Ceanannus Mór (translated as Main Head Fort) to distinguish it from the priory and town of the same name in Kilkenny, and eventually reduced to Kells. The sixteenth-century *Book of Howth* lists it among the five 'greatest towns of estimation that was in ancient time in Ireland' along with Derry and Armagh.

DIARMAIT AND COLMCILLE

Colmcille was a prince of the royal Uí Néill line, being a great-great-grandson of Niall of the Nine Hostages. He was trained as a druid and poet, eventually becoming one of the three most prominent Irish saints. He died in 593, and the graves of Sts Patrick and Brigit at Downpatrick moved apart to make space for him. Manus O'Donnell's 1532 *Betha Coluimb Chille* (Life of Colmcille) tells how Colm acquired Kells.

High King Diarmait mac Cerbaill lived at Kells. Colm went to visit him one day and was kept waiting at the gate. He whiled away the time by making prophecies about Kells, among which was that those who lived there then would not stay long. Then along came Bec mac Dé, the foremost seer of his time and Diarmait's personal prophet.

'Bec mac Dé,' said Colm. 'Make a prophecy about this place: will it be kings or clerics who live here?'

'It will be clerics,' replied Bec, 'and you will be the head of them, and never again will it be the place of a king.'

Diarmait was not at home at the time, and when he arrived he gave the whole town to Colm in compensation for having made him wait, and his son Áed Sláine agreed.

BOOK OF DURROW

The illustrated seventh-century volume of gospels called the *Book of Durrow* was probably made in England or on the Scottish Isle of Iona, but it was brought to Durrow Abbey in County Offaly some time before 916. There was a popular belief that Colmcille wrote it because the scribe named Colm who copied it signed his name. It subsequently went missing, and in the early seventeenth century the book, or part of it, was recovered from a Meath farmer who had been soaking it in water for its supposed miraculous properties, and using the water to treat sick cattle. This is part of an old tradition. Whatever came from Ireland was 'of Soveraigne vertue' against poison, according to Edmund Campion's *A Historie of Ireland* (1571). Drinking water with scrapings of books from Ireland cured adder bite.

BOOK OF KELLS

The eighth-ninth-century *Book of Kells* was called the Great Gospel of Colm Cille because it was written in honour of Colm on the bicentenary of his death. It was probably started on Iona and finished in Kells. The first historical reference to the book is in 1007, when it was stolen along with the jewelled box it was kept in and recovered wrapped in oilskin in a bog near Kells. The box, called a shrine, was never found.

CORMAC AND EITHNE

Kells figures in the tenth-century story 'The Melodies of Buchet's House'. Buchet was the owner of a bruiden, a royal inn known as Buchet's House, near Baltinglass in County Wicklow. He and his wife were fostering Eithne the Slender, a daughter of the high king Cathaoir Mór, and frequent and extended visits by her brothers and their retinues had left them in poverty.

Buchet complained to Cathaoir Mór, who said he couldn't tell his sons what to do, and he advised him to look for more modest accommodation. So Buchet and his wife and Eithne closed Buchet's House and moved to a small cottage in Kells.

Cormac mac Airt was living in Kells at that time, waiting for Cathaoir Mór to die so he could be king. He noticed Eithne as she went about her household chores and chatted her up.

'I notice that when you gather rushes for the floor and the bedding you collect them in three bundles: one with the best and two with the second-best. And when you draw water you fill two buckets from the edge of the river and one from the middle, where it flows clearest. And when you milk, you save the creamiest part in one bucket and the rest in the other two. Why is that?'

'I do that to honour one who deserves honour, and if I could do more to honour him I would.'

'Who is that?'

'My foster father, Buchet.'

'Are you Eithne the Slender?'

'I am.'

'Perhaps I can do something to help you give him that greater honour.'

So when Cathaoir Mór died, and Cormac eventually became king, he married Eithne. Since her father was dead, the bride price was due to her foster father. Cormac took Buchet to the ramparts of Kells and gave him everything he could see – not only the land, but also all the animals in view.

Buchet was now a wealthy man, and he and his wife returned to Wicklow and reopened Buchet's House.

THE MARKET CROSS

It is an old story still told – and possibly believed by some – that three of the high crosses in Kells were stolen by St Colmcille from St Kieran's church at Castlekeeran a few miles west of Kells. Having conveyed them to Kells, Colm was caught by Kieran trying to take another one. They struggled over the cross until Colm, unable to wrest it from Kieran's grasp, flung it into the nearby Blackwater, where they say it can still be seen.

High cross expert Helen Roe dismissed the story as 'malicious' and suggested that at least some of the crosses at Castlekeeran, which are of a different style from those now in Kells, might have been made in Kells.

One of the allegedly purloined crosses is next to the round tower in the grounds of St Columba's church and is often called 'The Cross of Kells', as if it were the only one in the town. Kieran and Colmcille stole it from each other so frequently that in the end no one knew whether it belonged to Castlekeeran or Kells. Helen Roe dated it to the eighth century. It has two other names: the South Cross and the Cross of Patrick and Columba. 'Columba' is the name Colmcille is known by in Scotland and is the version of his name often used for Protestant churches in Ireland. The twelfth-century East Cross or Unfinished Cross is also in the church grounds. Work on it is said to have been interrupted when the artist was killed in a Viking raid.

The Market Cross, ninth century according to Helen Roe, is now located in front of the Old Courthouse, at a safe distance from traffic and shielded from the worst of the weather by a plexiglass roof. It stood for many years in the market place where one of the gates of the monastic city used to be, at the junction of Cross, Market, Castle and John Streets, and that was probably more or less its original location. Some of the visible wear and tear is attributed to passing traffic, and records show that it was knocked down at least three times. At some point the upper part of the ring was broken off. An inscription on the shaft records its re-erection by Robert Balfe in 1688, and local tradition has it that Dean Swift set it in place again. In 1893 it was raised onto a plinth to protect it.

The Office of Public Works (OPW) had for a long time wanted to move it to a safer place, but the people of Kells circulated a petition demanding that it remain in situ. Part of their reasoning was that the market place was the most appropriate spot for the Market Cross, but there was an underlying belief that an unspecified 'something terrible' would happen to the town if the cross was ever moved.

In 1996 the plinth was hit and damaged by a school bus, though the cross itself was not harmed, and the OPW used that as an excuse to remove it from the busy intersection and take it into protective custody. It languished in storage until it was finally returned to Kells and installed in its present location in 2001.

THE TOWER OF LLOYD

Standing on the Hill of Tara, you can pick out Kells in the distance by its three towers. As you approach the town from Navan, the pointed spire next to St Columba's church and the round tower in the church grounds seem to form an intimate trio with the mile-distant lighthouse on the Hill of Lloyd. The late Benedict Kiely (1919–2007), born and raised in County Tyrone, novelist, journalist, broadcaster – whose mellow voice could charm with a recitation of the phone book – spins a yarn about that lighthouse in *Ireland from the Air* (1985).

At an agricultural show close to the town of Kells, and on the bountiful grasslands of Meath, a cub reporter from Dublin once asked a local veteran what was that there tower on the hill. He was told that

it was a lighthouse and later he began his story by mentioning the attractive seaside town of Kells.

It is tempting to assume that the cub reporter was none other than a young Kiely himself. The 100ft (30m) Tower of Lloyd, standing in what is now the People's Park, was built in 1790 by the 1st Earl of Bective as a private viewing stand to follow racing and the hunt.

FAIRY FORT AT DONAGHPATRICK

Near the church at Donaghpatrick between Kells and Navan is a mound thought to be a fairy fort. According to local tradition, there are underground passages in the area. A story current in the nineteenth century says that a group of young men and women entered one of these passages looking for fairy gold. They took with them a piper and a supply of whiskey to keep up their spirits. People outside could hear the piping until the sound came from under the church, and then it stopped. The young people were never seen again.

12

WEREWOLVES

The travel writer Gerald of Wales had a low opinion of Ireland and the Irish – 'a barbarous people' – and demonstrated his prejudices in the influential *Topography of Ireland*, first written in 1187 and amended and augmented throughout his life. On his visits to Ireland in 1183 and 1185 he amassed his material from first-hand observations, written sources and storytellers of varying credibility. The section of the three-part *Topography* titled 'Of the wonders and miracles of Ireland' displays examples of the timeless Irish practice of 'tell the tourist what he wants to hear.'

He would have come across the account that the Irish Nennius relates as the Fourteenth Wonder of Ireland: the people of Ossory, an ancient kingdom comprising parts of modern Kilkenny and Laois, can change themselves into wolves. If they are wounded in wolf-form the same wounds will appear on their human bodies when they change back, and if they are killed in that shape with flesh caught between their teeth from eating an animal, that flesh will be found between their teeth as humans.

On his way to the Siege of Limerick, George Story, chronicler of the Battle of the Boyne, heard about 'men in the County of Tipperary being turn'd into Wolves at a certain time of the year'.

This is a specific story, part quoted and part paraphrased, that Gerald tells about werewolves under the heading 'Of the wonders of our times: first, about the wolf who spoke with a priest'.

About three years before the coming of Lord John – King Henry II's son, later King John, who visited Ireland in 1185 – a priest and a boy were travelling from Ulster through Meath, and they camped overnight in a forest. They were sitting next to a fire under a leafy tree, when a wolf approached them and said urgently, 'You are safe. Don't be afraid when there is nothing to fear.'

The priest begged him by almighty God and by the faith of the Holy Trinity not to harm him, and to explain what sort of creature he was who in the form of a beast spoke human words.

'My wife and I are natives of Ossory,' said the wolf. 'Through a curse by St Natalis the abbot, a man and a woman of Ossory are made to take the shape of wolves every seven years for a period of seven years. If the couple survives, they are returned to human form, and another couple takes their place. Now my wife lies sick not far from here, and she is close to death. I beseech you to perform your priestly functions for her.'

The priest followed the wolf to a nearby tree, where he found a wolf moaning and lamenting. When she saw him, she greeted him and gave thanks to God in human language, and he administered the Last Rites. She asked him to give her Holy Communion, but he said he did not have any consecrated hosts with him. The male wolf pointed out the priest's missal in a pouch hanging from his neck, which contained a few hosts. When the priest hesitated, the he-wolf used his claws to peel back the skin of the she-wolf all the way from her head to her navel, exposing her human body. Seeing this, the priest gave her communion more out of fear than reason, and the he-wolf rolled back her skin the way it had been.

In the morning, the man-wolf led the priest and the boy to the correct road and thanked the priest for performing his office for his wife. Before they parted, the priest asked the wolf whether the enemy people who had conquered the island would stay here for a long time.

'Because of the sins of our people,' said the wolf, 'and the enormity of our vices, the anger of God has fallen on a depraved generation and given it into the hands of enemies. As long as the foreigners keep the commandments of the Lord and walk in His way they will not be overthrown. However, if they, by living among us, adopt our perverse habits, divine vengeance will be called down upon them also.'

Gerald appends an epilogue to the story:

Two years later, I happened to be passing through Meath when the bishop convoked a synod with neighbouring bishops and abbots to discuss the story the priest had told him about his meeting with the wolf couple. Hearing that I was in the vicinity, he sent two clerics with a message to invite me to the synod because of the importance of the matter to be discussed. The clerics told me the above story, which I had heard from others previously, but I had urgent business elsewhere and was unable to attend. However, I sent them a letter with the benefit of my advice. The bishop and the synod agreed with me, and they sent the priest, along with letters from the bishops and abbots, to tell his story to the Pope.

13

THE HILL
OF TARA

The Hill of Tara had five names. The first was Druim Decsuin, or the Conspicuous Hill; the second was Liath Druim, or Liath's Hill from a Firbolg chief of that name who was the first to clear it of wood; the third was Druim Cain, or the Beautiful Hill; the fourth was Cathair Crofinn; and the fifth name was Teamair, a name which it got from being the burial place of Téa, the wife of Eremon, the son of Milesius.

(From *Manners and Customs of the Ancient Irish*, Eugene O'Curry, 1873)

These are the three wonders of Teamhar, viz.: a youth of seven years of age begetting children; and the grave of the dwarf which measured five feet for every one, whether small or large; and the Lia Fail, i.e. the stone which shouted under every king whom it recognised in the sovereignty of Teamhar.

(From the Irish Nennius)

> Tara: every hill and height
> where stand ramparts and strong forts.
> Tara: every peak and crest,
> save far-famed Emain Macha.

> Shield of chieftains and heroes,
> home of valiant champions:
> nothing feeble, nothing faint.
> Tara: pleasing to women.
> (From *The Metrical Dindshenchas I*, Temair II)

A prose tale in the *Rennes Dindshenchas* says: 'Every conspicuous and eminent place, whether on a plain or in a house or wherever it may be, may be called by this word *Temair*.'

Most modern commentators seem to reason that since every high and conspicuous place is called Tara, the word 'tara' means 'high and conspicuous place'. I am told that my decidedly minority opinion that the word is cognate with the Latin *terra* (earth) is linguistically untenable. However, I offer in support two pieces of evidence:

1. The earth goddess associated with Tara, Maeve of the Red Side, shrieks under the true king through the Lia Fáil – a phallic symbol which penetrates the earth – to announce her approval, because the king is married to the land, i.e., the goddess of the land.
2. The Hill of Tara is the highest point on a long ridge. Tara is the name given to the highest point on a long ridge that forms a border between León and Galicia in Spain. Whether the Celts or any group actually came to Ireland from Spain, there are strong traditions linking the two countries, including trade stretching back to the Bronze Age.

I was on the Hill of Tara one day, when I saw a young Irish couple with their children come out onto the hill. The man glanced around, and, apparently because he saw no buildings, said, 'There's nothing here. Let's go.' And they went.

On the other hand, I took two young American women, Tara and Toni, to Tara. Tara was adopted. All she knew about her birth parents was that one was of Irish descent, hence her name. Before we arrived, I had populated the hill with stories of the gods and heroes and kings who are associated with the place. Once we got onto the hill, I simply pointed out what the various earthworks were and left them to absorb the atmosphere. They were in tears, overcome with the emotion of just being there.

Most visitors to Tara come because they are aware of the importance of the site. One notable example is Daniel O'Connell's Monster Meeting on 15 August 1843 (Lady Day), attended by some 500,000 people:

> We are on the spot [O'Connell said] where the monarchs of Ireland were elected; where the chieftains bound themselves by the sacred pledge of honour and the holy tie of religion to stand by their native land. This is the spot from which in ancient times emanated the social power, the legal authority, the right to dominion over the farthest extremes of the island, and the power of concentrating the force of the nation in national defence.

The *Cuimhnighimís ar 1798 i dTeamhair Brochure*, published in 1948 by the Tara '98 Commemoration Committee, comments: 'This was a notable gathering, too, in that the vast majority had fallen under the influence of Father Matthew. It was a strictly sober, orderly crowd.'

Nevertheless, archaeologists in the 1950s excavating the Mound of the Hostages, where the speaking platform was erected, discovered many empty whiskey bottles.

FIONN MAC CUMHAILL AND THE BURNING OF TARA

Cumhall of the Bascin clan was captain of the Fianna. Goll of the rival Morna clan killed him and became captain. When Cumhall's son, Fionn, reached the age of manhood, he came to Tara and demanded of King Conn of the Hundred Battles that he be named captain of the Fianna. This was a problem for Conn. If he made Fionn captain, the Morna clan would rebel. If he didn't, the Bascin clan would rebel. Either way, there would be war within the Fianna.

There was only one way out of the dilemma. Conn explained to Fionn that Aillén came out of the Otherworld entrance at Tara, the passage tomb called the Mound of the Hostages, every Oíche Shamhna (Halloween). He played music on his magic flute to put everyone to sleep and burned all the buildings. Even Goll was unable to stop him. The captaincy of the Fianna was Fionn's if he could put an end to Aillén's depredations.

Fionn's father had bequeathed to him a bag of magic treasures. One was a cap of silence: if he put it on with the flaps covering his ears, he wouldn't be able to hear Aillén's sleep music. Another was a spear named Birga, which had once belonged to Aillén. The story that might explain how Cumhall got it and why Aillén was burning Tara has been lost. The spear loved the slaughter so much that it had to be kept chained to a wall with its head in a bucket of water wrapped in leather; otherwise, it would run amok and kill everyone within reach.

The next Oíche Shamhna, Fionn waited with the cap of silence and the spear. When Aillén arrived and played his sleep music, Fionn couldn't hear him because of the cap. He confronted Aillén with the spear, and when Aillén saw his own spear in Fionn's hand, he ran 50 miles overland to his own Otherworld entrance at Sídh Fionnachaidh – Deadman's Hill north of Newtownhamilton in County Armagh.

Just as Aillén was entering the sídh mound, with one foot in the Otherworld and one in this world, Fionn threw the spear and killed him. He cut off his head and brought it back to King Conn. That's how Fionn mac Cumhaill saved Tara from burning and became captain of the Fianna.

FIONN AND GOLL AND THE GIANT

A great giant came to Tara from a foreign land and demanded tribute or a fight with 100 men from Cormac mac Airt. He got three fights and killed 300 of Cormac's warriors. Cormac called on Fionn mac Cumhaill and the Fianna. The giant killed 100 of the Fianna.

Fionn asked Goll mac Morna if he would care to take on the giant in exchange for a third part of the spoils and a bonus, and Goll agreed. They fought all day, and when they stopped at nightfall, Fionn came to the giant in the guise of a storyteller and offered to tell him stories with the condition that he would not fall asleep while he was telling. The giant agreed, and Fionn yarned all night. The giant fought Goll again the next day, Fionn kept him awake all night again, and the same the following day and night, so that finally the giant was so tired he lost half his strength, and Goll killed him.

FIONN AND CÚCHULAINN

After he died, Fionn mac Cumhaill appeared to his son Oisín and told him that he had been sent to Hell. He said that the Devil ordered the rest of the Fianna to attack him, but the Fianna, led by Fionn's arch-enemy Goll mac Morna, attacked the demons of Hell instead, in spite of the fact that Fionn had wronged the Morna clan many times.

'After sixty years,' Fionn said to Oisín, 'the King of Heaven had mercy on me and sent an angel to tell me to leave Hell for one night to visit you. Go to the place where Cúchulainn is buried. Heaven will be given to you by the King of Heaven from the Day of Judgment onward.'

Tara is one of the places where Cúchulainn's head and right hand are said to be buried. At St Patrick's request, Cúchulainn appeared to King Laeghaire and Patrick at Tara 400 years after his death to try to persuade

Laeghaire to become Christian, which Laeghaire did nominally but not in truth. However, for his efforts, 'Heaven was decreed for Cúchulainn.'

At the end of their lives, Oisín and his cousin Caoilte met with St Patrick on the Hill of Tara and were baptised by him. Patrick christened them Art and Conn.

WHY THE FIELDS OF MEATH ARE CLEAR OF STONES

One of the most haunting stories of the Otherworld is that of Midir and Étaín. To summarise: Midir and Étaín fell in love and got married. Midir's first wife put a spell on Étaín that sent her far away. Étaín eventually returned as a human and married High King Eochaid Aireamh (of the Plough), having forgotten her life as a sídh woman. Midir challenged Eochaid to play fidchell (like chess) – the winner to name his prize – and lost two games. One of the prizes he had to give to Eochaid was to clear all the stones out of the fields of Meath. He did this by harnessing horses with collars, so they could pull the stones efficiently. (The stone-free fields of Meath testify that this story is true.) The usual method had been to tie ropes to the horses' tails. Eochaid copied Midir's innovation for ploughing, hence his sobriquet.

Midir won the third game and demanded Étaín as his prize, and, in the versions that end the story there, they lived happily ever after.

MODERN STORIES

I stopped with a group of Dutch members of OBOD (Order of Bards, Ovates and Druids) at a whitethorn tree near the top of the ceremonial entrance road and explained its significance. Some people who recognise the power points in the body called chakras say that Tara is the heart chakra of Ireland, and that tree is the heart chakra of Tara. Another belief holds that the guardian spirit of Tara resides in that tree. The OBODs immediately sat down and held an impromptu ceremony in honour of the tree and what it represents.

A friend of mine named Al Cowan, a musician, recording engineer and member of the Society of Irish Reenactors, went to Tara late one Halloween night with his fellow Reenactors in their medieval Irish costumes to have a quiet party. Al was painted blue and wearing a cloak and carrying a spear.

He left the group to visit a whitethorn tree that he is especially fond of, in the valley off the west side of the hill. As he approached the tree, he could hear harp music, which sounded louder the closer he got. He stopped and stared when he saw a petite blonde woman wearing tights and a short green dress with wings on her back, playing a small harp. She felt him looking at her and stopped playing to stare back at him.

'Are you real?' she asked.

'I was about to ask the same thing about yourself,' he replied.

It turned out that she was an Australian visiting friends in Navan. They had also decided to have a party at Tara, and she had likewise left her group to play her harp under a tree that she seemed to feel a special relationship with.

It's part of the magic of Tara that each of them thought for a moment that the other might be a visitor from the Otherworld on a night when the gates between the worlds are open, especially at Tara, where the Mound of the Hostages is one of those gateways.

14

THE CURSING OF TARA

High King Diarmait mac Cerbaill had a steward named Baclam, who travelled around the country visiting local and provincial kings to make sure they were keeping the peace. His method was to carry a spear crossways through the front gates of their castles. If the entrance was too narrow, it meant that the king was at war with a neighbour or at least expecting trouble, and Baclam, in the name of the high king, demanded that the entrance be widened as a way of cooling tempers. This was a rough but effective shortcut to forestall violence and at the same time enforce Diarmait's authority. One account of this story puts a sinister spin on Baclam's actions. According to the section on St Ruadán in Charles Plummer's *Lives of Irish Saints*, Baclam was a 'vile and outrageous person' who acted 'at the instigation of the devil'.

Baclam paid a visit to the castle of Áed Guaire, king of Uí Maine – south Roscommon and southeast Galway – and tried to enter with his spear. The gateway failed the test, and Baclam ordered it to be demolished. The servants did so, but when Áed Guaire found out, he killed Baclam. Knowing that he was in serious trouble for killing Diarmait's steward, he fled to Muscraige in Tipperary to be under the protection of his half-brother Bishop Senach.

Senach was afraid of the power of Diarmait and took Áed Guaire to his foster brother Ruadán. Ruadán was of the royal blood of Munster.

He studied at Clonard, and when he finished he went to Muscraige and then founded a monastery at nearby Lothra. Many wonders are attributed to his intercession, including the casting out of demons, healing, and miraculous provision of food and drink.

Ruadán was also afraid of Diarmait's anger, and he took Áed Guaire to Britain. When Diarmait heard of this, he went to the king of Britain and demanded that he give up the refugee. Áed Guaire returned to Ireland and again sought protection from Ruadán, who concealed him in a chamber beneath his oratory at Pollrone in Kilkenny. Diarmait discovered that the fugitive had returned and sent his charioteer to Ruadán to demand the surrender of Áed Guaire. When the charioteer approached the oratory he was struck blind and did not return to Diarmait. Suspecting a problem, the king himself went to the oratory and asked Ruadán where Áed Guaire was, confident that the holy man would not lie to him.

'I don't know where he is,' Ruadán replied, 'unless he is under my feet.'

Diarmait left but had second thoughts about the ambiguous answer and sent a servant to search for an underground room. As soon as the servant began digging, his hand withered so that it was useless, and he also did not return to Diarmait. (The servant and the charioteer later became monks and saints.) As a divinely appointed king – Adomnán says he was 'ordained by God's authority as ruler of all Ireland' – Diarmait was immune to harm, and he dragged Áed Guaire from the chamber and took him to Tara.

Ruadán gathered the rest of the Twelve Saints of Ireland, and they followed him to Tara and sang psalms of cursing and rang their bells so forcefully against him that they damaged the bells. That night, the twelve sons of the twelve kings who were staying at Tara died. The kings complained to Diarmait, saying it was his fault. The foster fathers of the dead boys pleaded with Ruadán to restore them. The holy men prayed *crosfhighil* (cross-vigil: kneeling with arms spread in the form of a cross), and God brought the boys back to life.

Then the holy men fasted against Diarmait, an ancient method of forcing the powerful to accede to a plaintiff's demands, which was regulated by strict rules under the Brehon laws, unlike its modern equivalent, the hunger strike. Convinced of the justice of his arrest of Áed Guaire, Diarmait fasted against the saints, which was his legal prerogative. The fasting duel went on for a year, during which the participants were permitted to eat every second day. Then Ruadán offered to ransom Áed Guaire and asked Diarmait what he would accept. Thinking he was setting an impossible demand, Diarmait said he would take fifty blue-eyed horses in exchange for Áed Guaire.

At this time, St Brendan of Clonfert happened to be traversing the sea, and an angel came to him and revealed that the saints of Ireland were in trouble and explained the problem. Brendan landed in Connaught, rounded up fifty seals and turned them into horses, and brought them to Ruadán, who presented them to Diarmait. Diarmait set riders on the horses to try them out, and when they put

whips and spurs to the beasts they ran off with the men into the Boyne and turned back into seals. Some men were drowned and others only saved themselves with difficulty.

Diarmait demanded compensation for the death of his men, but Brendan came up with another trick. It was a day when the saints were not supposed to eat, and he told them to bring food and drink to their mouths but dump it into their robes, and then pretend to be chewing and drinking. Diarmait saw this and assumed they had broken their fast, and so he broke his, which meant that legally and morally he had lost the fasting duel.

Diarmait had a dream: twelve men cut down a mighty tree with axes. The sound of the tree falling woke him up, and he understood that the tree was his kingship and the axemen were the saints. All he could hear was the constant cursing and bell-ringing of the holy men. In the morning he went out to speak to them. He said he was only trying to maintain justice and order and peace, and he accused the monks of bringing the law into contempt and protecting criminals. Then began the cursing match, which can be summarised thus:

Diarmait: 'Your Church will be the first to fall.'

Ruadán: 'Your reign will fall sooner, and none of your descendants will be kings.'

Diarmait: 'Your place will be deserted.'

Ruadán: 'Tara will be desolate forever.'

Diarmait cursed Ruadán with the loss of an eye, a foot and a hand, and this was eventually fulfilled. Ruadán retorted that the ridge beam of the king's own house would fall on his head and kill him and that he would die by wounding, burning and drowning (see chapter 8), and his body would be scattered after death. That was also fulfilled: his head was buried at Bective Abbey and his body in Kildare. Finally, Diarmait surrendered with the parting shot: 'Even though all Ireland be at peace, may thy Church's precinct be a scene of war continuously.' The story-teller concludes, 'And from that time to this the same is fulfilled.'

A poem attributed to Diarmait begins: 'Woe to him who contends with the clergy of the churches.'

15

ACHALL
(THE HILL OF SKRYNE)

An alternative modern spelling is 'Skreen'. The Irish word is *scrín*, meaning 'shrine', from the Latin *scrinium* and cognate with the Old Norse *skrin*, which may be the origin of the 'k' in the modern anglicised place-name.

In the thirteenth-century French poem called in English 'The Song of Dermot and the Earl', which tells of the Anglo-Norman Conquest, Earl Richard of Pembroke (Strongbow) distributes Irish properties to his loyal followers:

> *E Scrin ad pus en chartre,*
> *Adam de Feipo l'ad pus doné.*
> [And Skreen he then gave by charter:
> To Adam de Phepoe he gave it.]

Achall was the daughter of Fedelm, daughter of Conor mac Nessa, King of Ulster. She was buried on the hill and is memorialised in the old name for the Hill of Skryne.

When Cúchulainn was killed in the Field of Slaughter south of Dundalk, Achall's brother, Erc, cut off his head and buried it at Tara. Conall Cernach and Cúchulainn had agreed that whichever of them was killed first, the other would avenge his death before sunset. When

Conall heard that Erc had cut off Cú's head, he pursued him to Dublin and removed his head and buried it at Tara also.

When Achall learned of her brother's death, she 'came out of Ulster to bewail her brother. For nine days she kept at the lamentation, till her heart broke in her like a nut, and she said that her grave and her burial mound should be in a place from which Erc's grave and burial mound would be seen. Hence are named *Dumae n-Eirc* and *Dumae n-Aicle*.' (*Rennes Dindshenchas*, translated by Whitley Stokes.)

CORMAC MAC AIRT AT ACHALL

When High King Cormac mac Airt was blinded in one eye and therefore ineligible to remain in the kingship, he retired to Achall and wrote a code focusing mainly on criminal law called *The Book of Aicill*, which was revised and updated by the seventh-century king Cennfaeladh the Learned. That book and the *Senchas Már*, which deals with civil law, can be seen as companion texts of early Irish law. Both are cited in *Ancient Law* (1861), a standard work in international law by the eminent English jurist Henry Maine.

ST COLMCILLE AT SKRYNE

> There came to Temair of the kings
> Colum Cille free from sorrow;
> by him a church is founded there
> on the hill where Achall was buried.
> (*The Metrical Dindshenchas*, translated by Edward Gwynn)

There was no well, so Colm prayed, and a clear fountain burst forth. He pounded iron nails into a stone that is still visible at the well. When Colm died in 593 on the Scottish island of Iona, where he had founded a monastery after his expulsion from Ireland, he was buried there. It is called *Ì Chaluim Chille* in Gaelic. But after devastating Viking raids forced the monks to flee and close the monastery, some or all of his remains were transferred to Ireland and divided between the monastery at Kells, which he had founded, and Skryne, which takes its modern name from *Scrín Cholmcille*, the Shrine of Colmcille. The word 'shrine' nowadays usually refers to a structure, but in this case it was a container for Colm's bones. The *Annals of the Four Masters* report for 875: 'The shrine of Colum Cille, and his relics in general, were brought to Ireland, to avoid the foreigners [Vikings].' But in 1127: 'The shrine of Colum-Cille was carried off into captivity by the foreigners of Athcliath, and was restored again to its house at the end of a month.'

The Ghosts of Skryne

Sir Bromley Casway owned Skryne Castle in 1740. A wealthy neighbour named Phelim Sellers, a widower whose wife had died under suspicious circumstances, lusted after Sir Bromley's young ward and distant relative, Lilith Palmerston, who lived at the castle. When his advances were spurned he attacked her in the garden, but servants intervened. Later, when he learned that she was about to leave for Dublin to get away from his attentions, he attacked her again in her room and killed her. One account says that he choked her by stuffing foxgloves down her throat. He fled but was soon captured and hanged.

Lilith's screams have been heard since then, and the ghostly figure of a young woman clad in white is sometimes seen running from the house, clutching her throat. A stout man dressed like a squire of the eighteenth century has also been spotted.

St Patrick at Skryne

James Neill of Navan, aged 74, told collector D.F. O'Sullivan in 1938: 'I often heard the old people saying that St Patrick fell asleep upon the Hill of Skryne and he took the brogues off to rest his feet, and when he wakened he hadn't them. They were stolen and they were sold in Tara for the price of a drink!' (NFC 580:68)

16

CÚCHULAINN AT CROSSAKEEL AND ÁTH N-GABLA

As Queen Maeve of Connaught was marching with the combined armies of the 'men of Ireland' to invade Ulster in search of the Brown Bull, in the epic *Cattle Raid of Cooley*, Iraird Cuillenn – Crossakeel – lay on their route.

Cúchulainn and his human step-father, Sualdam, were standing watch on the hill there, grazing their horses around a pillar stone. Sualdam's horse cropped the grass to the soil, and Cú's horse cropped it to the bedrock. Cú told Sualdam to go and warn the Ulstermen to stay out of sight and avoid Maeve's armies, as he himself had a date that night with warrior-woman Fedelma of the Nine Beauties, daughter of King Conor of Ulster and (later) wife of Loegaire Buadach. Or perhaps it was with her handmaiden; the manuscript sources are ambiguous. Sualdam disapproved: 'Woe to him who goes thus and leaves the Ulstermen to be trampled underfoot by their enemies and by outlanders for the sake of going to a tryst with a woman.'

Cúchulainn replied that he had to honour the arrangement; otherwise, women's accusations that men are unreliable would be verified, so he was doing it for the benefit of all men. Anyway, he had time for romance because his presence wasn't needed immediately. He had a plan to obstruct Maeve's progress, to delay the armies until the Ulster warriors could recover from Macha's nine-night curse that had left them as weak as a woman in childbirth.

He went into the woods and cut an oak sapling with one stroke of his sword, tied it in a knot with one hand, with one eye closed and standing on one leg – the ritual used for the dreaded *glam dícend* curse – and forced the hoop down over the top of the standing stone until it encircled the base. He fastened it with a peg and inscribed on it a description in ogam of what he had done, putting Maeve's army under *geis* (prohibition) not to pass it without stopping to camp for the night. Then he went to his tryst.

When the invading army arrived and found the message, Ailill, Maeve's husband, asked the Ulster exile Fergus what it meant. Fergus interpreted:

> If ye do not spend a night here in encampment until one of ye makes a similar ring, standing on one foot and using one eye and one hand as Cúchulainn did, even though that hero be hidden underground or in a locked house, he will slay and wound ye before the hour of rising on the morrow, if ye flout his condition.

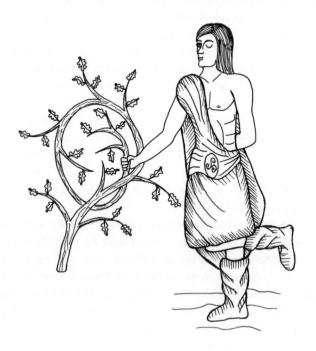

No one could duplicate the feat, of course, so the armies were forced to bypass the sapling and Cúchulainn's *geis*. They turned off the road and cut down trees to make a path for their chariots, hence the name Slechta (*slechtad* = hewing), which is now called Kilskeer, and proceeded to Kells, where they spent the night in a heavy snowstorm.

The following day, Cúchulainn woke late after his night of trysting and discovered that the invaders had passed him, so he rushed ahead of them and stopped at a ford called Áth n-Grena over the River Mattock at Beloch Caille Móire (Kellystown) near Mellifont Abbey north of Slane. He went into the woods and with one stroke of his sword cut a sapling that had four prongs on it, sharpened the end and charred it for hardness, and then wrote a message in ogam on it. He threw it from the back of his chariot so that two-thirds of it went into the ground in the middle of the road, leaving no room for a chariot to pass on either side. All done with one hand.

Two forward scouts preceded Maeve's forces, Err and Innell, with their charioteers Fráech and Fochnam. Cúchulainn cut the heads off all four of them and impaled them on the four-forked pole, and he sent the horses back to the armies with the bodies in the chariots. For that, the name of the ford was changed from Áth n-Grena, the Gravelly Ford, to Áth n-Gabla, the Ford of the Fork.

Fergus interpreted the ogam for the warriors: 'It is *geis* for the men of Ireland to go into the bed of this ford until one of ye pluck out the pole with the tip of one hand even as he drove it in just now.'

Ailill asked him who had planted the pole, and Fergus told him it was his and King Conor's foster son, Cúchulainn na Cerdda, the Hound of Culann the Smith, and he predicted ill fortune for those who continued on the quest for the Brown Bull.

'Heroes will be cut in pieces by the baneful sword of Cúchulainn. No easy gain will be his strong bull for whom a fight will be fought with keen weapons. When every skull has been tormented, all the tribes of Ireland will weep. I have no more to say concerning the son of Deichtire, but men and women shall hear of this pole as it now stands.'

As an Ulsterman, and not one of the 'men of Ireland' to whom the *geis* applied, Fergus pulled the pole out of the road with his chariot, and the invaders moved on into Louth.

17

HOW THE RIVERS NANNY AND DELVIN GOT THEIR NAMES

This delightful description of the Nanny comes from the *Atlas and Cyclopedia of Ireland* (1900):

> The Nanny Water runs south of, and parallel to, the Boyne, at a distance of 3 or 4 miles; it rises a little east of Navan, flows the whole way along a beautiful valley, and passing by Duleek, falls into the sea 4 miles south of the mouth of the Boyne.

The Delvin River – An Ailbhine – is officially classified as a stream. It runs along the Meath-Dublin border for much of its length, meeting the Irish Sea north of Balbriggan near Gormanston. (Not to be confused with the Devlin – An Duibhlinn – near Slane, flowing into the Mattock and thence into the Boyne.)

When the men of Ulster decided it was time for Cúchulainn to get married so he wouldn't be tempted by their daughters and wives, he set off with his charioteer, Laeg, to Lusk in County Dublin to court Emer, daughter of Forgall the Wily. (The story of the Wooing of Emer – Tochmarc Emere – was written down in the eighth century.) It was ostensibly a social visit in a group setting. Their conversation was conducted in intricate, metaphorical language to prevent Emer's sisters and the others from understanding what they were talking about, because they both knew that Forgall would oppose their marriage. Emer started by asking a variant of the usual 'How was your journey?'

Cúchulainn meticulously detailed his itinerary using literal forms of place-names in a way designed to put listeners off their guard, so that when he gazed lustfully at Emer's bosom and commented on the beauty of the 'plain of two yokes' it sounded to the eavesdroppers like just more tedious topographical description.

Cú's listing of landmarks included '*for tonach ech nDéa*' and '*for Ollbine*'. On their way back to Ulster, Laeg asked Cú what the words meant that he and Emer were using, because they obviously made little sense on the surface. Cú mentioned crossing the Boyne (see chapter 34) and then:

> '*For tonach ech nDéa*,' I said: 'Over the Washing of the Horses of Déa,' that is, Ange [River Nanny]. The Washing of the Horses of Déa was its name originally, because in it the Men of Déa washed their horses when they came from the battle of Moytura. It was called Ange after the king whose horses the Tuatha Dé Danann washed in it.

To explain the meaning of '*for Ollbine*', Cú told the story of how the Delvin got its name:

> Rúad son of Rigdond son of the king of Fir Muirig [the People of Magh Muirigh, i.e., Moymurthy north of Gormanston near Mosney] set off in three ships crewed by thirty men in each to visit his foster brother in Norway. The ship was brought to a sudden halt in the middle of the Irish Sea. They threw jewels and other valuables overboard, but nothing they did could make it move. Rúad jumped into the sea and saw nine women, three under each ship, who were the most beautiful in the world. They told him they had stopped the ships to make him stay with them. They carried him off, and they gave him nine vessels of gold to sleep with all of them for one night each, sometimes on dry land and other times on a bronze bed. At the end of that time, one of the women said that she was pregnant, and they only allowed him to continue his voyage on

condition that he would return to them on his way back to Ireland.

He spent seven years with his foster brother in Norway, and on his homeward journey he made sure to avoid the spot where he had met the women. But they discovered that he had detoured around them, and they pursued him in their bronze ship. When Rúad and his people reached Inver Ailbine, the harbour at the mouth of the Delvin, they heard martial music coming from behind them:

> Sweet the song those women cried,
> sweet and mellow was their sound,
> chasing Rúad with their prow
> o'er the vigorous streaming tide.

As the women sailed their ship into the harbour, one of them threw her and Rúad's son out of the boat so that he landed on a rock and was killed. Then all the women and Rúad's people cried out, '*Ba holl, ba holl in bine!* – It was heinous, it was heinous the crime!' (Hence Ollbine/Ailbhine.)

The prose is my rewrite of Kuno Meyer's 1888 translation. The above stanza is from 'Inber n-Ailbine' in *The Metrical Dindshenchas*, which goes on to recommend that the plain near Gormanston be named for the 'stout pillar' Muiredach son of Cormac, which may be the origin of Moymurthy (Irish: *Maigh Muiri*). This might be the Muiredach son of Cormac from Slane, who was Abbot of Louth and died in 758, according to the *Chronicle of Ireland*, a tenth-century chronicle that no longer physically exists but survives in later copies called 'daughter chronicles'. The *Annals of Ulster* say a man of the same name, a superior of Dromiskin in County Louth, died in 912. Cúchulainn's telling of the story is the source of the Dindshenchas versions, which could have been composed as late as the eleventh or twelfth century.

GARRAWOG

Her name was Maura Gargan, also called the Cailleach Geargain, but she is known as Garrawog in the story. 'It was said that she lived at Tierworker, some place about the foot of Tierworker Mountain,' Michael Gaffney of Relaghbeg, Mullagh, Kells, told collector P.J. Gaynor in 1941:

> She was going to Mass in the old church at Moybologue. She told her servant man to get her a blackberry. He refused, as everyone went fasting to Mass in those days. She got down off her horse and plucked the blackberry herself. And when she ate it she ate the man and the horse. Saint Patrick was sent for, and only he killed her by throwing his staff at her she would have eaten the congregation.
>
> I used to hear it said that where Saint Patrick slew Garrawog, one part of her was buried in the hollow of the road near Mick the Brock Gargan's. (This would be on the road from Relaghbeg to Tierworker, and which passes the ancient cemetery of Moybologue.) There are big flags of stone in the road at the place where she (or a quarter of her) is said to be buried. It was stated that Saint Patrick said she would rise again when nine times nine, or it might be 199 or 999, generations of Gargans had been taken that way for burial at Moybologue. [Some say when 999,999 Gargans

had walked over the spot. One version has the woman change into a 'ferocious black swine'.]

And I remember when I was a little boy seeing funerals of Gargans leaving the road when they came near to the spot and going into Sheridan's field and coming out on the road again further on. They were afraid that if they crossed the spot she would rise again. They said that another part of her went into Clugga Lake.

(NFC 792:259-61)

A separate account says that another quarter of her went up into the air and another east into the sea. Sheridan's field is just across the road from the new cemetery.

O'Donovan, in the Ordnance Survey of 1836, made a few guesses at the meaning of the town/townland in northwest County Meath on the Cavan border called Tierworker ('Teevurcher' on the map): *Taobh Urchair* – 'side of the great cast or throw or for practicing missile throwing', 'land of great tillage', 'Murcher's house'. *Taobh* literally means 'side', but it is also used for 'site', and 'site or place of the cast' ties in with Patrick's throw of the crozier, though the story may have come about to explain the place-name, as many of the Dindshenchas yarns do. Kathleen Cooney of Tierworker told me that *Taobh an Urchair* refers to an old tradition of holding sports competitions on Tierworker Mountain. 'There was a traditional fair, and at the fair there was missile throwing or skittles, and it was known for tournaments of skittles – the place of the missile throwing.'

Moybologue is where Fiacha Finnfolaidh, king of Ireland, was killed in AD 56 in a revolt by vassal tribes. His son, Tuathal Techtmar, mentioned in the Introduction as giving Meath the name of Meythe, gained the kingship twenty years later by killing the rebels' king in the Battle of Achall.

THE BACHALL ÍOSA

Garrawog was a powerful witch or demon, and so a more powerful weapon was needed to defeat her. What better instrument than the staff that Jesus had carried?

On His travels, Jesus stopped one time on an island in the Tyrrhenian Sea (an arm of the Mediterranean west of Italy) and was given hospitality by a young married couple. He blessed their house and said that they and the house would remain young and new until Judgment Day. He left His staff there, telling them that St Patrick would drop by in a few hundred years to collect it. Just before he came to Ireland as bishop, Patrick visited the island and found that same couple, as young as ever, with old and decrepit children and grandchildren, and they gave him the staff.

This was the famous Bachall Íosa, which found its way into many – often irreverent or sacrilegious – hands down through the centuries. Gerald of Wales said in the twelfth century that it was the most famous and potent of all the saints' croziers in Ireland, and St Patrick used it to banish poisonous reptiles. It was moved from Armagh to Ballyboghill in County Dublin, thence to Christ Church in Dublin in 1173 and preserved there until 1538, when it was stripped of its gems and gold covering and publically burned in High Street by the Archbishop of Dublin, George Brown.

CLUGGA LAKE

Clog, the Irish for 'bell', or *clogán*, 'small bell', could be the origin of the name of this lake, which is at Relaghbeg, southwest of Tierworker. It was drained about twenty years ago and has nearly disappeared. Teddy McCabe of Tierworker told me: 'If you got out there and peered your eyes down in the valley, you might see a puddle of water. That's Clugga Lake.'

St Patrick founded a church in Moybologue, and in Penal Times the bell was removed and thrown into Clugga Lake, according to Barney Gargan of Tierworker:

> And every seven years that bell was heard ringing below in the lake. The late James Reilly, of Annacloo, who died about forty years ago [before 1941], often said that he heard the bell ringing in the lake and that there was always an interval of seven years between each time it rang.
>
> (Collector P.J. Gaynor, NFC 792:454)

> Long years ago there was a man buried in Moybologue graveyard, and because he had done something that made him unpopular his body was lifted and left outside the graveyard gate. The police came and buried it again. It was lifted a second time, and was buried again. But the third time it was lifted it was carried away, and I used to hear the old people saying that it was thrown into Clugga Lake.
>
> (Daniel Lynch, 69, Leitrim, Mullagh, Moynalty, collector P.J. Gaynor, 1941, NFC 792:408-9)

Folklorists will undoubtedly find it a fascinating challenge to work out the mythological significance of the demon Garrawog, the bell of St Patrick's church, and a 'riz' body all ending up in Clugga Lake.

19

A Ballad of Moybologue

This ballad was composed about the 1920s. The author is believed to be Peter (Peetie) McConnon of Coppanagh.

'Tis said when Saint Patrick first blessed our land
On the moat of Moybologue our saint took his stand.
He blessed Relaghbeg and likewise Relaghmore,[1]
He looked on Blackhills, said he'd bless no more.
And turning his features towards heaven he cried,
'Shall I bless such a place? I don't think I will,'
And weeping he turned away from the hill.

'Twas the time th' influenza was sweeping the country,
Taking a like to the poor and the gentry.
Jack Flanagan stole into town in October.[2]
He drank a few bottles, but still he was sober.
He stuck in his pocket a bottle of rum
To be ready in case th' influenza might come.
He strolled home again singing songs of green Eireann
And his shouts could be heard the far side of Cairn.[3]

The night it grew dark and would you believe it,
He passed his own turn and didn't perceive it.
All the ditches he crossed he swore were past counting,
Till he found himself climbing the side of the mountain,
When a light from a window attracted his eye.
'What villain lives here?' our hero did cry.
He knocked and he shouted, to open the door;
When he got no response he kicked it in on the floor.

And there was poor Mitchell sitting up in his bed
With a jar to his feet and a rag round his head.
'Ara, how are you Jack? I'm glad you came in.
For the past three weeks I've been down with the Hen.[4]
And the devil a neighbour ever put in his head
To see if poor Mitchell was living or dead.'

Jack says to Jemmy, 'You're a horrible sight,
You would frighten a ghost in the dark of the night.
Didn't you stay out all night card playing
When you should have been home in your old cabin praying?
And you lay in your bed till ten in the morn
When your cows were eating and tramping people's corn.
Your stole Barney Weirns' shirt and drawers too,[5]
And you sold them for nine pence to Brian the Blue.[6]

'It's the way nature built you, the fault's not your own;
Jemmy, she gave you a heart like a stone.
The heart of a miser she placed in your breast;
Mitchell you couldn't be much at your best.
You have a mind like a knitting needle narrow and long.
It's taught you to do everything crooked and wrong.

'Now, Jemmy, you'll soon see Beelzebub here at your bed
With a map in his hand of the life that you led.
All your past deeds down your throat he'll keep stuffing.
Hell to your soul, 'twas your cow was the roughin.'[7]
'Twas said through the window ole Nick would go flying
Whenever Jack Flanagan called on the dying.

When Jack was going home, he bid him 'good night'.
From around the corner, what caught his sight
But a pair of long horns from behind an old chair.
Jack wasn't long guessing the devil was there.
He took off his coat and threw it one side
And straight for the candlestick it happened to glide.
The candle and candlestick flew out of sight
And left the two lads in the dark of the night.

At this point, poor Flanagan flew into a rage.
'You have come here already your battle to wage.
You can take Barney Weirns by the scruff of the neck
Or humpy Pat Andy to hell if you like.[8]
You can slip up to Rowntrees for Mussey or Pritchill,[9]
But damn it to hell if you'll get Jimmy Mitchell.'
Jack roared at Jemmy to kindle the light,
And he'd soon put an end to this one-sided fight.

At this stage poor Mitchell got terribly perplexed,
For he knew that his own turn would surely come next.
And as he was trying to crawl out of the tick
Jack drew out wild with a box and a kick.
And the last words he heard as he shot through the door
Was 'Take him to hell, but don't hit me no more.'
At this time poor Mitchell vacated the bed,
And the blanket and sheet he pulled round his head.

He sprang down the mountain, a perch with each bound.[10]
His speed was ne'er reached by the Countryman's hound,
 Till he came to the cottage of Owen McEntee,
 And there from the beginning he told his story.
 Owen sat listening and spoke not a word.
Sometimes he thought 'twas a nightmare he had
And more times he was partly believing the lad.

 Owen said, 'Sit down there until the cock crows,
  And then with you to your cabin we'll go.
 When we see the appearance of things at your cot
  We'll soon ascertain if you're raving or not.'
 The two boys sat there until the cock crew,
 And with sticks and a lantern started the two.
When they reached Jemmy Mitchell's they found such a sight
 'Twas enough to give them a terrible fright.

There were chairs without legs and legs without chairs.
 The clothes and the blankets were bundled in layers.
There was large pools of blood here and there on the floor
 And the face of the wag-of-the-wall at the door.[11]
The wheels and the weights were scattered over the ground,
 And a trace of the pendulum never was found.
There was large cakes of plaster which happened to fall
When Jack missed the devil and hammered the wall.

 As the sun it was rising o'er Agheragh's height
 To quench the last struggling resemblance of night,
 Mitchell found a puck goat in the street in the morn
 With blood on his hooves and Jack's shirt on his horn.

Commentary by Philip Donnelly, with contributions by Teddy and Peter McCabe and Richard Barber. Philip remembers hearing this ballad being recited during his childhood in Tierworker in the 1930s and '40s. I found it on his blog at http://www.donnellycanada.com/tierworker/arts-recreation/100-moybologue-moat-dance.html . Used here with permission.

NOTES

1. Relaghbeg, Relaghmore and Blackhills are a few of the townlands around the ancient cemetery and the Moat of Moybologue.
2. Bailieborough, 3 miles away in County Cavan, was probably the town Jack stole into.
3. The Cairn is the highest point on nearby Loughanleagh Mountain.
4. The Spanish Flu of 1919 was known as the 'Hen'.
5. Barney Gargan, nicknamed Barney Weirns, lived a short distance down another lane not far from Mitchell's.
6. Brian Donnelly was a son of Bridget Donnelly, nicknamed Biddy the Blue.
7. 'Your cow was the roughin' no doubt means that Mitchell's cow was one of the roving kind – a ruffian – with no respect for fences.
8. 'Humpy Pat Andy' was Pat Clarke, who helped Philip Donnelly's father Jemmy Donnelly of Greaghnadarragh rebuild the old Donnelly house.
9. Mussey and Pritchill were two deserters from the British Army who lived and worked with John Rountree of Coppenagh for several years.
10. A 'perch' is a length of five-and-a-half yards, i.e. 5.03m.
11. The 'wag-of-the-wall' was a style of clock mounted on one of the walls of the kitchen. It operated with a pendulum and weights.

20

TAKEN BY
THE FAIRIES

These stories, preserved in the National Folklore Collection, are similar to reports of abductions by fairies elsewhere in Ireland.

There was a young child playing on the bog where they were cutting turf, but she fell into the bog hole and was lost in it before the people saw her. This bog I heard was Bohermeen [the Jamestown Bog, near Navan], but I cannot rightly tell you.

The mother was at home in the house. The people did not rise her out of the bog hole until they told the mother about it, and when the mother heard the news she asked them what did they do with her. They said they did not rise her until they'd tell her, and she told them not to interfere at all with her, to leave her there.

And they left her so, and the mother sat up that night and at one o'clock the child walked in to her and she says, 'You are the best mother anyone ever had. Only for you I was gone.'

The child was all right and there was an old broom or besom got in the bog hole that appeared to be the girl to the people. The child was brought away with the fairies and if the people had taken up what appeared in the bog hole and buried it for the child – it appeared like a child – the fairies would have the child, and all that they were burying was a besom. The charm was broken by them leaving what they believed to be the child in the bog hole.

I heard several stories of things like that. I think it was an aunt of mine I heard saying it. She is long dead.

(James Caffrey, Jamestown, aged 60, told to
D.F. O'Sullivan, 1938, NFC 580:102)

There was a man lived in the town of Trim one time and they lost a child. I don't know whether it was lost or died but it appeared to the father and asked its father to go such a night to this sheep path and that she – the little girl – would be the eighth that would come out on the gap and to seize her and hold her. But the man failed and she never appeared to him any more. I am hearing that story as long as I remember. The old people used talk about it. They used be blaming this man as he didn't go.

(James McCormack, Gilltown, aged 91, 1938,
collector D.F. O'Sullivan, NFC 580:75)

Long years ago there was a house in our back field, and a man named Mylie Reilly was living in it. One evening his daughter went out to bring home the ducks, and, lucky enough, she happened to bring the tongs with her. She was putting the ducks out of the river when she was seized by the 'gentry'. They brought her 'a mile of ground' but they had to let her go because she had the tongs with her. She was half the night away and her people were out looking for her. She was all torn by bushes and briars when she got back home.

(Barney Gargan, Tierworker, collector
P.J. Gaynor, 1941, NFC 792:447)

21

THE THREE DEATHS OF FIONN MAC CUMHAILL

It would be irrelevant to swell these pages by quoting the innumerable passages we could extract from ancient authors of unquestionable authority to show that the Fenians did exist.

(Nicholas O'Kearney, 'The Battle of Gabhra',
Transactions of the Ossianic Society, 1853)

In a strange echo of the Threefold Death (see chapter 8), in which a king is killed by wounding or poison, fire and drowning, there are three very different versions of how Fionn died.

ASSASSINATION – AD 283

Fionn was a military dictator, and the Fianna were his private army, through whom he was able to enslave the people of Ireland and intimidate even the high king, according to some accounts. The usual view is of Fionn as a great hero and the Fianna as the guardians of the land, even when mention is made of certain privileges those elite warriors enjoyed. They supported themselves by hunting from April to October but were billeted on the people for the rest of the year. No woman could marry until the warriors of the Fianna had been asked three times if any of them wanted her, which meant she had to endure the humiliation of three rejections.

Moreover, the Fianna demanded a right called *mercheta mulieris*, which like its companion or alternative custom, *jus primae noctis*, is encoded in Latin because of its distastefulness. The *mercheta* was a payment a man had to give to the lord in order to let his daughter marry: a sort of wedding licence. The Fianna demanded that it be paid to them, usurping the traditional right of the king. It would not be surprising if the Fianna also demanded the *jus*, the right of spending the first night with a newly married bride. Some sources say it was the *mercheta* that sparked the Battle of Gabhra-Achall in 284, in which the Fianna was destroyed. Others say the issue was salmon.

It was a privilege too far when the Fianna ordered that no one could take game – salmon, birds or animals – even if they were found dead, except themselves. Fionn was living on the banks of the Boyne and apparently had a salmon-weir. Three local fishermen attacked Fionn with their gaffs and killed him, and three warriors of King Cairbre beheaded him. Fionn's grandson Oscar then led the Fianna against Cairbre in the Battle of Gabhra-Achall in revenge.

DEATH BY MISADVENTURE

The members of the Fianna noticed that Fionn was growing old, and they drifted away until only one was left.

''Tis true then,' said Fionn to himself. 'It is old age the men notice on me. I shall test that by my running and leaping, for it is in the east my "Leap" is, on the Boyne, and I shall go to its brink.'

It is believed that kings, especially the high kings, were required to undergo some sort of physical test annually to assure their subjects that they were still able to lead them. As one of the seven kings of Ireland – the high king, the four provincial kings, the king of the poets, and Fionn as the king of the Fianna – Fionn regularly tested himself by leaping across the Boyne on stepping stones at Áth Brea (still called 'Bray' in the eighteenth century) at the Broadboyne Bridge near Stackallan. But this time he failed. The fifteenth-century *Book of Fermoy* reports:

Thereupon he fell between two rocks, so that his forehead struck against the rock and his brains were dashed about him, and he died between the two rocks. Fishermen of the Boyne found him. They were four, the three sons of Urgriu, and Aiclech the son of Dubdriu. [Fionn had killed Urgriu, who had killed Fionn's father.] These found him, and Aiclech cut off his head. And the sons of Urgriu slew Aiclech. They took Fionn's head with them into an empty house, and boiled their fish, and divided it in two. His head was over against the fire.

'Give it a morsel,' said an evil-jesting man, 'since Aiclech is no more.'

Three times the fish was divided in two, and each time there were three portions.

'What is this?' said one of them.

Then said the head of Fionn from before the fire:

> ''Tis this that has caused the third division:
> That you haven't given me my bit.'

KILLED IN THE BATTLE OF GABHRA-ACHALL – AD 284

High King Cairbre, son of Cormac mac Airt, gave his daughter in marriage to a prince without consulting the Fianna, who expected, as their privilege, to be offered first refusal. Also, Cairbre had previously asked Aideen to be his wife, but she turned him down in favour of Oscar, son of Oisín, son of Fionn mac Cumhaill. A contributing factor to the battle was surely the death of Cairbre's three sons in the Battle of Cnámros in the *Bórama* saga, when the Fianna were allied with the Leinstermen against him.

The sixteenth-century manuscript, Egerton 1782, describes the final battle of the Fianna in overwhelming detail – 'Now when the manful, puissant, powerful, terrible, fierce-battling prince of the Fianna, and the valorous, fierce, combative hero, even Cumhall's son of many battalions beheld that battle-phalanx arrayed against him …' – but it can be summarised thus:

Fionn had killed Goll mac Morna, and Goll's grandson, Fer-lí, who was Fionn's foster son, stirred up the old feud between his clan and Fionn's. With a force of 4,000, including the 'ancient tribes' of Tara, Fer-lí attacked Fionn and the Fianna and their allies, who numbered only 500. At the end, Oscar and Cairbre killed each other, Fionn was seriously wounded by Fer-lí and his father before killing them, and then the five sons of Urgriu speared him simultaneously and killed him.

Gabhra-Achall is the area between the hills of Tara and Skryne and stretching to the south.

Some say Fionn was away in Rome at the time of the battle, and he wept when he heard of Oscar's death. Then he died as related in one of the versions above. That was only the second time he had wept for a person; the first was when Sadhbh, the love of his life and the mother of Oisín, was taken away to the Otherworld by the Dark Druid. He later also wept at the death of his favourite hound, Bran.

THE ALTERNATIVE ENDING

On the other hand, a persistent tradition has it that Fionn, like Earl Gerald and Red Hugh O'Donnell, lies sleeping in a cave with members of the Fianna and the Trumpet of the Fianna. Someday, a man will stumble upon the cave and blow three blasts on the Trumpet, and Fionn and the Fianna will awake and rise again as strong as ever. Meanwhile, Lady Gregory reports in *Gods and Fighting Men*:

> And as to the great things he and his men did when they were together, it is well they have been kept in mind through the poets of Ireland and of Alban. And one night there were two men minding sheep in a valley, and they were saying the poems of the Fianna while they were there. And they saw two very tall shapes on the two hills on each side of the valley, and one of the tall shapes said to the other: 'Do you hear that man down below? I was the second doorpost of battle at Gabhra, and that man knows all about it better than myself.'

22

GATES
THAT WON'T
STAY CLOSED

A neighbour of mine when I was living in Avoca, County Wicklow, the late Hughie McCusker, told me this story in the 1980s. Hughie was a fine natural storyteller from Rathfriland, County Down. I assume he heard the tale from a resident of Moynalty, possibly when he attended a Steam Threshing Festival.

It was well known that the gates of a Big House outside Moynalty were always closed in the evening but were always found open in the morning. *Something* opened them after midnight.

One night, a group of lads were returning from the pub in a car after midnight. As they passed the Big House one of the passengers, fortified with Guinness courage, said to the driver, 'Stop the car. Them gates are open. Back the car and shine the headlights on the gates. I'm going to close them bloody gates so they stay shut.'

The driver manoeuvred the car so the lights illuminated the gates. Our hero got out, marched to the gates and closed them and fastened them with a heavy iron bar. He came back to the car, dusting his hands in triumph and said, 'Now, I'd like to see anything open them bloody gates.'

The wide-eyed, pale-faced driver said, 'Well, then, you'd better look now.'

He turned around and saw that the gates were already opened. Hughie said that the man nearly went through the side of the car trying to get into it.

Danny Cusack of Kells consulted a friend in Moynalty and said she confirmed the story and said that the house is Westland House, a couple of miles south of Moynalty on the road to Kells. Danny said, 'The place was owned by the Barnes family for generations but is now vacant. My friend also mentioned that after Mrs Barnes died the locals were disappointed that the thing about the gates staying open did not hold true.'

The late Tommy Murray of Trim told a related tale in his 2006 book, *Meath Voices*. Local pranksters closed a gate one night that had never been closed, and in the morning the postman, expecting to find the gate open as usual, was killed when he drove into it. That was the story that was circulated, but it never happened. Someone was only playing a grisly trick on the lads who had closed the gate. Tommy said it was Niblock's Gate on the Navan Road from Trim.

A similar story is found in Conor Brennan's *Yellow Furze Memories*, where he mentions a gate in Yellow Furze that was closed at night but found open in the morning.

23

THE SPEAKING STONES

The Speaking Stones in the townland of Farranagloch (Quarter of the Stones) in the field called Pairc-na-gclochalabartha (Field of the Speaking Stones) northwest of Oldcastle fell silent about the year 1800. From time immemorial they had been reliably consulted by people whose cattle had strayed or whose milk or butter had been bewitched or who were the victims of thieves. They were also said to be helpful in settling disputes.

E.A. Conwell, in his 1873 book *Discovery of the Tomb of Ollamh Fodhla* about the passage tomb cemetery on the Loughcrew ridge, explained:

> It is even yet current that they have been consulted in cases where either man or beast was supposed to have been 'overlooked'; that they were infallibly effective in curing the consequences of the 'evil eye'; and that they were deemed to be unerring in naming the individual through whom these evil consequences came.
>
> Even up to a period not very remote, when anything happened to be lost or stolen, these stones were invariably consulted; and in cases where cattle, &c., had strayed away, the directions they gave for finding them were considered as certain to lead to the desired result. There was one peremptory inhibition, however, to be scrupulously observed in consulting these stones, viz. that they were

never to be asked to give the same information a second time, as they, under no circumstances whatever, would repeat an answer.

William F. Wakeman (*Handbook of Irish Antiquities*, 1891) reported:

These conditions having, about seventy or eighty years ago, been violated by an ignorant inquirer who came from a distance, the speaking stones became dumb, and have so remained ever since.

P. Martin gave the details in *The Breifny Antiquarian Society Journal*, I, II, 1921:

A pilgrim who had a bad memory once came from afar to the venerable stones. He put his question and duly received his response. But, unfortunately, the very next minute, before he had right set out for home, he forgot the answer. Turning on his steps, and totally unmindful of the dread 'geis' or prohibition, he repeated the question.

Conwell:

Wroth with indignation at this open violation of the terms upon which they condescended to be consulted, the Speaking Stones have never since deigned to utter a response.

Wakeman described the stones:

Two of these relics (there were originally four) of a long, long past are at present extant. The larger may be described as consisting of a thin slab of laminated sandy grit. Its dimensions are as follows: total height above ground, as nearly as possible, 7 feet; extreme breadth, 5 feet 8 inches; breadth near summit, 3 feet 6 inches; average thickness, about 8 inches. In no part does it exhibit the mark of a chisel or hammer.

The height of the second remaining stone, above the present level of the ground, is 6 feet 4 inches; it is in breadth, at base, 3 feet

4 inches, and near the top 1 foot more; thickness at base, 14 inches. The material, unlike that found in the generality of such monuments, is blue limestone.

The two stones remain in the field, but one now lies flat on the ground. One of the standing stones in Cairn L on Carnbane West on the Loughcrew ridge is called the Whispering Stone, leading to confusion among commentators.

24

THINGS YOU
MIGHT MEET
ON THE ROAD

Some of the following stories are first- and second-hand and factual,
others are hearsay, but they all have one thing in common: you never
know what you might meet on the road, day or night.

The first story was told to me by Marion Gilsenan of Kells:

When my auntie Eileen was a girl she used to visit her aunt in the
local village of Mullagh around a mile away from her own home.
On this particular winter evening when she was setting off home after
her visit, her aunt accompanied her out the road a bit because there
was a group of young fellas hanging around at the top of the town.
After parting from her aunt she walked out the dark road on her own.

After a while she heard footsteps behind her but took no notice
because she thought it was a neighbour who'd catch up with her
and walk along. When no one seemed to be catching up she became
uneasy and quickened her footsteps, thinking it might be one of the
lads from the town following her. The other footsteps quickened
too, and as she walked along she felt a hand on her shoulder and
the footsteps beside her. No one spoke. She was so scared she didn't
dare look behind her but continued to walk rapidly. When she got
to a crossroads – Watty's Cross – within a quarter-mile of her own
house the hand left her shoulder and the footsteps stopped. She ran

the rest of the way home. She told the story and the consensus was that someone had played a joke on her and she was gullible enough to fall for it.

As time went on she forgot about her experience. Grew up, left school and went to England to train as a nurse. When about six or seven years later she returned to Ireland and a job in a local hospital, she came home for the weekend and drove to a dance where she met up with her then boyfriend and future husband.

After the dance was over she set off home alone. After only a few miles, her car stopped. It had run out of petrol. She considered returning to her boyfriend's house but decided that she was more than halfway, and as she was working the next day, there was nothing for it but to walk home, maybe 6 or 7 miles.

She set out and made good headway, and as she was beginning to flag she realised that she had come to the turn-off for her road, just before the village of Mullagh. She turned up the road, walking rapidly, knowing that she would soon be able to fall into bed. And then! She heard footsteps behind her! She didn't turn around. She said later that she knew by the way the hair stood up on her neck that this was the same encounter. She walked along, heart in her mouth and suddenly, there it was again. The hand on her shoulder! She couldn't look behind, just sped up as the hand and the footsteps sped up beside her. Once again they disappeared around Watty's Cross and she hurried home to bed.

Interestingly, there was always an old story told that one should beware of the Long Man when in the vicinity of Watty's Cross.

This story is told by Jack Hand's son, Malachy, from Oldcastle:

On a bright winter's night, Jack Hand and his friend John Hennessy were returning home across the fields to Millbrook Mill, near Oldcastle, after playing cards. As they entered a certain field, a tall man dressed in a long black coat walked beside them, and when they crossed into an adjoining field the tall man disappeared. Nobody spoke until he left, and then one said to the other, 'Did you see that?' Both had experienced the same sight.

When they related their story and described the tall man to some old people they said it was the last of the Quaker Webbs and that he was buried inside the grand gates of nearby Castlecor House, where there was a Quaker graveyard. This incident happened in the early twentieth century.

This graveyard causes some confusion, as it is noted in Larkin's 1812 map as a Jewish graveyard, although tradition suggests it was Quaker, and this story often told by Jack Hand backs up this folklore.

This was told to collector P.J. Gaynor by his father, James, of Edengora, who died in 1926 aged 81 (NFC 792:290-1):

One night I was returning home from Moynalty, and when I came to Rathsteen a black man stopped me on the road. I tried to get by him, but he kept in front of me on the road and wouldn't let me pass. I turned back and when I was near Moynalty I met a man that I knew, and told him what had happened. He said, 'I will leave you by the spot.' He came back with me and left me by the place where the black man stopped me. We saw nothing, and I met or saw nothing on the rest of the way home.

This story was told by Peter Rogers, 47, Newtown, Kilmainhamwood, to P.J. Gaynor in 1941 (NFC 792:105a-106a):

> One night I was in a hotel in Slane and was preparing to go home. A man said to me, 'I wouldn't like to pass Blackbourne's gate at Tankardstown.' I asked him why, and he said that old Blackbourne might catch me. I said that I didn't believe in that sort of thing at all. He then told me the following story. One night a number of men, including the late Frank Ledwidge, the famous poet, were in a public house. Some of the men said that old Blackbourne was seen standing at his own gate on the previous night. Others replied that he had been often seen there. Frank Ledwidge said he would go down and talk to him if they'd agree to accompany him.
>
> The men were more or less afraid but after some persuasion they consented to go with him. They all set out together and when they came within a short distance of the gate there was Blackbourne standing beside it. Ledwidge went over to the ghost and said, 'What takes you here frightening the people?' The ghost made no reply, and Ledwidge said, 'Go to hell or wherever you've come from.' The ghost immediately turned into a ball of fire and disappeared.

This account was told by Annie Barber of Killagriffe, near Tierworker, where she lived from the age of 12, in a radio interview on 12 April 1997 when she was 91. It was transcribed by her son Richard. She died in 1999. I found this on Philip Donnelly's blog, The Tierworker Ceidhle House, at www.donnellycanada.com. Philip is from Tierworker and now lives in Ottawa, Canada. The story is used here with the permission of Richard Barber and Philip Donnelly:

> I never seen a ghost, I did, I seen one. I'll not say it was a ghost but I'll not say it was anything, but it was something. We was coming [back to Killagriffe] from Church in Bailieborough one night and a boyfriend with me and me brother Dick, and we came to a certain place down there on the road, and says the boyfriend to me, he says, you have Dick with you now – this was on a Sunday night maybe about eight or nine o'clock – so you will be all right going home

and I'll go back. We had three bicycle lamps on our three bicycles, when here we seen this thing coming up the road and it came as close to me as that, and she was a big tall round woman and her two feet coming out bare from under the gown, and her white hand holding the mantle round her head and she was just as near to me as you. We all spoke, but she never spoke, so we stayed on a few minutes and come to the decision that we'd come on, we'd pass her coming down the road, but we never passed her. That was the only thing ever I seen that I never knew what it was.

James Caffrey, 60, Jamestown, told the following story to D.F. O'Sullivan in 1938 (NFC 580:106):

[A blacksmith named Smith looked out of his forge on the Kells road one day.] What was coming up the road only a funeral and very few people with it, and he made up his mind to give them a lift for a bit, and it was about 2 miles from Athboy. He thought they'd let him out somewhere up the road before they'd come to the town with it. They never let him go, and they went through the streets of Athboy and a mile outside the town before they let him off, but as he was going up the street a lot of the kids of the town – gossins and geirshas [boys and girls] – all began to cheer and bawl and followed him up the street saying, 'Oh, look at the man going up the street and the bookalawn [rag-weed] on his shoulders.'

An uncle of mine Jimmy Connor who is dead 40 years [in 1938] and was 70 years at the time told me that story.

The following account is from 'Irish Folklore from Cavan, Meath, Kerry, and Limerick' by Bryan H. Jones in *Folklore*, Vol. 19, No. 3, 1908. The author gives his source as Mr H.T. Radcliff 'from Boylan'. 'Dullahan', as the headless driver is often called, is apparently an Anglo-Hibernicism created to apply only to this creature. It probably derives from *dallacán*, meaning a completely blind person, with the influence of *dubh* to denote a dark creature that is headless and therefore blind. The Dead Coach (*cóiste bodhar* = deaf or silent coach) is sometimes described as silent, other times as making the same sound as an ordinary coach.

の

The main *raison d'être* of the Dead Coach, as it is called in Louth and Meath, with its headless driver and headless horses, seems to be to give notice of an approaching death in a certain district, or among the members of some particular family. For instance, there are Dead Coaches at Kilcurry and Ardee, in Louth, that appear when anyone in the parish is about to die; while at one place in Meath there is a Dead Coach that is never seen except the night before the decease of the local squire or one of his relations. There is a Limerick family which enjoys a similar privilege. In their case the Headless Coach drives up to the hall door, and on arrival there every seat save one is seen to be occupied by the ghost of an ancestor.

There is, however, another function of the Dead Coach, as the following tale from Meath shows. Some years ago there died a large landowner, Mr Y., who had made himself popular with the country people by giving land to enlarge an ancient graveyard that was situated on his property. According to them he was so fond of the place that he gave directions that he should be buried there, but when he died his relations said that no gentleman had ever been buried at T_____, so they laid him to rest in the churchyard in a neighbouring town.

The night after the funeral, as a labourer named Barney Boylan was on his way to the town, he heard the rumble of a carriage behind him on the road and stepped aside to let it pass. The sound passed him by, and he could hear it proceeding along the road in front of him, but he could see nothing. Presently the vehicle seemed to stop in front of a gate, but when he drew near it went on again. Boylan turned and made for home, where his wife asked him what the carriage was that had passed the cottage going towards the town. While they were talking the carriage passed by in the opposite direction, 'tattering up the road for all it was worth.' Another woman heard the same sounds that night. It was the Headless Coach bringing Mr Y.'s body to T____.

25

CROMWELL

The effects of the Cromwellian occupation are well remembered in Meath:

A woman walking along the street in Duleek passed a group of Cromwell's soldiers, and one of them killed her. Cromwell was angry at that and asked the soldiers which one of them had killed the woman. No one answered. He said, 'I will give the highest post in Drogheda to the man who killed her.' A soldier admitted that he was the one. Cromwell had the man taken in a cart to Drogheda, where he was hung from the top of the Tholsel.

(Richard Connor, 76, Commons, Duleek, collector
Seán Ó Concubair, 1938, NFCS 0682:248)

Local tradition has it that Cromwell camped on Crossakiel hill, and that he offered 1,000 acres of Clonabreany [about 3km west of Crossakeel] to one of his officers who had distinguished himself in the fighting. But the officer, looking down on the valley, said: 'I wouldn't live in an old swamp like that.' Then up spoke a Drummer Boy and said: 'I would be delighted to own 1,000 acres of such land,' and Cromwell said: 'Young Wade, I'll give you 2,000 acres.' The Wades flourished in the place for nearly 300 years.

(Beryl Moore, 'Exploring Clonabreany', *Ríocht na Midhe*, III, 3, 1965)

The Cruise family held large tracts of land in Meath and other counties, one of their mansions being Cruicetown, between Nobber and Kilmainhamwood, but they were dispossessed of their lands by the Cromwellians, their bodyguard routed, and the head of the family residing at Cruicetown had to 'fly for his life'. He concealed himself in the flags [grass-like plants] and reeds of Cruicetown Lake. The soldiers were searching for him and as they approached the spot where he was concealed, a crane, with an eel in its mouth, rose up from the waters beside him and flew away. The officer in charge immediately recalled his men and said it would be useless searching there – that the crane would have cleared away the moment that anybody came about the place, and that consequently the fugitive could not be hiding there. The crane saved his life, and in commemoration of the incident an engraving of a crane, with an eel in its mouth, may be seen on the Cruise tombstone in Cruicetown graveyard to the present day.

(Peter Rogers, 47, Newtown, Kilmainhamwood,
collector P.J. Gaynor, 1941, NFC 792:112-113)

26

THE 1798
REBELLION

In the weeks following the decisive defeat of the 1798 rebels at Vinegar Hill in Enniscorthy, a large number of men from Wexford and Wicklow, joined by some from Kildare, moved into Meath to continue the fight. A group of about half a dozen asked for food and shelter at a farm owned by a man named Morgan. He fed them and told them to go into the loft in the barn to sleep, and then he notified the local yeomen. They killed all but one of the sleeping rebels by thrusting their bayonets up through the floor of the loft, which was woven of willow.

The lone survivor, a 20-year-old Wexford man, leapt from the barn and ran across a field. However, he did not get far: he was shot and wounded, then finished off with bayonets. A week later, his mother came to claim his body, which she found mangled and torn and being eaten by a sow belonging to Morgan. She cursed Morgan and his farm, and local tradition says that the curse remains effective to the present day. Morgan went mad, the succeeding owner lost all his wealth and committed suicide, the next went mad, the next failed and sank into drink, and so on.

The following story was told to Seumas O Gormain for the Schools Collection in 1938 by Liam O Gormain, aged 60, Commons, Duleek (NFCS 0682:197-8):

About a hundred years ago the Irish were fighting against the English on the Hill of Tara, and one of the Irish was hid in a cock of hay near Athcarne Castle, waiting for the English to come. After a while he could see them coming up an old lane. The minute he saw them coming he began to fire at them. But he had not many bullets and he had to use the buttons of his coat.

The English were not afraid of this, so they came up and set the cock of hay on fire. And when the Irishman came out they killed him and buried him in the same place. Soon after a tuft of thistle grew up like a headstone to mark the place where he was buried, and every night he can be seen standing there and he will go away the day that Ireland is free.

DEATH OF FATHER MURPHY

In retreat after the second Battle of Tara, September 1798, Father John Murphy was leading his Wexford contingent north in the direction of Nobber. At a bridge on the border of Mountainstown and Drakestown north of Wilkinstown they encountered yeomen, who fired at the priest at close range. He caught the balls in his hands and threw them back at the attackers, saying that no one would be able to kill him except a member of his own religion.

As it happened, one of the yeomen was Catholic, and he ran at the priest and slashed him in the neck with his sword. Father Murphy went to the stream and washed his wound before dying. (Paraphrased from *Cuimhnighimís ar 1798 i dTeamhair Brochure*, Tara '98 Commemoration Committee, 1948.)

MOLLY WESTON, HEROINE OF TARA

Molly Weston, from Fingal near Oldtown, County Dublin, and her four brothers took part in the 26 May Battle of Tara. She was described by survivors as being dressed in green with gold braid, wearing a green cocked hat with a white plume, and riding a

white horse. The British soldiers were experienced and disciplined professionals with modern weapons; the Irish the opposite. Also, one of the local landowners paid for three wagons of whiskey to be delivered to the rebels, and some took full advantage of the gift. As the battle went against the rebels, Molly rallied and encouraged them, repeatedly leading charges. The rebels managed to capture a field gun and turn it on the British. Molly dismounted and fired the gun herself.

No one witnessed her death in battle, and she was not found among the dead or captured rebels. A white horse bearing a side-saddle was found dead on the battlefield afterwards, but Molly Weston was never seen again.

WHERE THE WHISKEY CAME FROM AT THE BATTLE OF TARA

Murphy the Distiller in Navan went around by Tara with a horse load of whiskey – oh, he was bribed to do it – and they took the whiskey and got drunk and lay about and the English came and stuck them like pigs.

So he made his way home as best he could, avoiding Bective Bridge and all the bridges on the Boyne, because he was told they were all guarded. He came between Trim and Bective Bridge by Thompson's of Rathnally, and Thompson [a Protestant] told him not to attempt any of the bridges, that they were all guarded. Thompson gave him a horse and told him to swim across the Boyne with him. Their lawn is just sloping for the Boyne. He told him to turn the horse in the river and that he'd swim back, and then he gave him advice to put the pike in the first ditch he'd meet.

So he came home and his father and mother were crying hearing he was killed in Tara, so he went into Athboy [and all the Protestants] ran to shake hands with him, but he told them that he wasn't in Tara at all. He denied being in it.

(Told to collector D.F. O'Sullivan by Pat Martin,
Jamestown, in 1938, NFC 580:107)

27

BURIED ALIVE

A vault to the south of the Saint Oliver Plunkett church in the Loughcrew Historic Gardens bears the name of William Jones of Newtown. The date appears to be 1743. The wife of this Jones got a weakness one evening, from which she did not appear to recover, and it was presumed she was dead. In due course she was interred in this tomb. She seems to have been a very beautiful woman, fond of dress, and especially jewellery. She always wore a magnificent diamond ring, which had to be buried with her as it could not be removed without cutting off the finger.

They seemed to be in good circumstances, for they always kept a butler to attend the family at meals. This butler, knowing all about the family, had, like his mistress, a great admiration for diamonds, so the night after the funeral he decided that he would recover the diamond ring at any cost. He provided himself with the necessary implements to open the tomb, and the coffin as well, with a sharp knife. He opened the tomb and the coffin, saw the famous ring on his mistress's finger, and at once proceeded to remove it by cutting into the flesh.

As soon as he did, the blood began to flow. His mistress moved and opened her eyes and made a piercing scream. The butler bolted, leaving the ring and his mistress in the vault, and the story tells us he was never heard of again. The lady got out of the coffin and, in her grave clothes, appeared at Newtown, to the surprise and no little horror of her family.

(From 'Loughcrew from the Early Days',
John McDonnell, *Moylagh Community Centre
and St. Oliver's Park Official Opening*, 1983)

The fact that very similar incidents with specific names, locations and dates have been reported from the United States, most European countries (nineteen in Germany) and elsewhere in the days before embalming does not necessarily mean that this story is not true. The most famous such burial in Ireland is that of Marjorie (or Margorie) McCall of Lurgan, whose tombstone in Shankill Cemetery reads 'Margorie McCall – Lived Once, Buried Twice'.

28

LOUGH SHEELIN
LOCH SÍODH LINN –
LAKE OF THE FAIRY POOL

Phil Lynch, 82, Rathmore, told these two stories to collector
D.F. O'Sullivan in 1938:

Lough Sheelin is an enchanted lake. My father was often telling me
that there was a little copper skillet in his aunt's house, where he lived
for six years over six miles from the lake. When the sun was shining
on the calm waters of the lake the people thought they could see
houses below on the bottom. An uncle of my aunt's was a swimmer
and diver, and for two years he was threatening to dive down and
see if it was a fact. So he collected some men on horseback in case
anything would happen – to take him away – and he dived in.

When he got to the bottom of the lake he met with a little street
of houses, and the first house he met he went into it. Well, there
was an old woman sitting in the corner and she combing her hair,
and when he came in the door she just threw the hair out of her eyes
and looked at him, and she says, 'Ye bloody villain, what brought
you here?' He told her that he often threatened to come down when
they'd see the houses when they were boating.

'Well,' she says, 'away with you back as fast as your heels can
carry you. You may thank goodness that the lads are not within or
you'd never get back.'

'Well,' he says, 'if I go back without some token they won't believe me.'

There was this little pot that I was talking about standing there.

'There's a poteen there. Bring it back with you. The lads will be in about one o'clock, and if they catch you in the water you will never get back.'

So he hooked it off, and the fellows on the shore watching him and they loaded with silver because they couldn't shoot an enchanted thing with any other. So there was a horse waiting for him as soon as he left the water. Then the others that were on watch saw the heavy waves coming in the water, so he went away on the horse, and the others stood watching. There came a huge big fish up out of the water and was gaining on the horse, and when he was riding the fish went out on the land and the horse was a good one by all accounts and on full gallop. One of the fellows that was on watch fired at the fish and wounded him, and it turned back, and every slash of his tail tore up the ground like a plough. He got into the water and it turned all red with his blood.

I heard my father and mother telling that story a thousand times. He heard it from his aunt. My father often had that little pot in his hands.

When tourists would be coming to the lake she had the little pot there to show it to them. There are people living below in that lake just as they are living here. That fellow that went down to the lake never went near it any more. He was in terror day and night and never got any health until he went away out of the country.

I don't know what became of the little pot after my father left his aunt's house at the age of nine.

I have another story about Lough Sheelin. I was told it for a down-right fact. Well, this young fellow was a farmer's son and very fond of fishing. He lived convenient to the lake, and he used be very fond of going out fishing in a boat, and he often wondered how it was that, on a fine day and the water as calm as possible, it would get rough in a hurry with no wind.

He went to college to study for the civil service. On this one occasion he was home and as usual he went out one day to fish on the lake with a line and hook and a gaff, and he saw this big fish in the water. He oftentimes had a narrow escape of being thrown by it before. He thought it was too big for his line, so he gaffed it. But the fish was so big and so strong it nearly capsized the boat before the line broke. So the fish got away and the young man went home.

Five days later he was in the parlour studying when it seemed to get dark, and he raised his head and saw a young gentleman standing in the doorway who called him by name.

'You have the advantage of me,' he said. 'I don't know who you are, but you seem to know me.'

'I often saw you when you didn't see me,' he said. 'Do you remember the day you were out fishing and were very nearly capsized by a big fish?'

'I do.'

'Well, that wasn't a fish. It was a young girl. She's my sister, and she was in love with you. Those other times you nearly capsized, that was the girl trying to get you into the water. If she could get you into the water you'd be hers. That girl is lying in a house at the bottom of the lake, and she is very ill because your gaff is stuck in her jaw. If you don't come down and take the gaff out she'll die.'

So the young student said, 'I'll do it to save her life, if you'll promise that nothing will happen to me.'

'Nothing will happen to you. I'll leave you back here safe.'

The student went to get a bathing suit, but the stranger said it wasn't necessary. When they arrived at the lake and walked into it, the student expected to meet with water, but there was no water. He remarked on this to the stranger, but he only smiled and told him not to mind.

Soon they could hear the moaning of the girl, and they went on till they came to some houses, and in either the first or second house they went into, the mother – and I think a sister and a second brother – were there at the door and welcomed them and showed them into the room where the girl was lying in bed with the gaff stuck in her jaw. They told him that if he took it out she'd get well at once, and as quick as the gaff was taken out she was perfectly well again. So the joy of the world was there with them, and they thanked him for coming down.

The girl then reminded him of all the times when the water got suddenly rough, and she said that was herself trying to get him into the water so he'd be hers because she was in love with him, and she asked him to marry her. He said he'd marry her if she came to live on the land. She said, 'If I did that, at the first sight of the water I'd leave you, and it would only make you miserable. But if you consent to marry me and live here we could make our lives happy.'

He wouldn't agree to that. As they parted, she told him that if she ever got the chance to get him into the water he'd be hers.

Her brother walked with the student back to the shore, and as before there was no water. When they arrived at his house, the merman disappeared.

(NFC 580: 109-113)

29

CURES AND
SPELLS

About seventy years ago there lived near Oldcastle a farmer named Morris O'Connor. He had a brother a priest. Morris had the name of 'dealing in witchcraft' – he could make 'cures' – and for that reason the priest was not on friendly relations with him. One day as the priest was coming along the road his horse fell, and all efforts to make him rise proved a failure. Vets were sent for, but none of them could diagnose his ailment.

Somebody suggested to the priest that he should send for Morris; his reverence would not consent, but in the end Morris was sent for without the priest's consent. Morris arrived, put his hand on the horse's shoulder, and told him to get up. The animal immediately got up, shook himself, and proceeded home. There was not a bother on him after that.

About the same period there lived at Feagh, near Moynalty, a farmer named John Smith, a brother of Bernard Smith, a famous rural poet. John had a bullock that was ailing for a couple of years – it was a 'piner'. Vets and local quacks tried to cure him but failed. Smith heard about Morris O'Connor and his reputed skill in matters of the kind. He did not know him personally, Oldcastle, where Morris lived, being about twelve miles away.

One morning early Smith set out for Oldcastle and arrived at O'Connor's home. Morris opened the door and said, 'Good man, John Smith from Feagh, how are you doing?'

Smith was greatly surprised by the manner of the greeting – he had never met Morris before and Morris had never met him. Smith looked at him and said, 'How do you know me?'

Morris replied, 'Why wouldn't I know you? Aren't you comin' to me to get your oul' pine of a bullock cured? If you had come to me long ago you'd have saved yourself a lot of trouble and expense. But I'll go over tomorrow and leave him all right.'

On the following day Morris arrived at Feagh and made a cord with knots on it. He then put the cord around the bullock's neck, after which it got up and wasn't a day sick as long as it was about the place.

> (Peter Rogers, 47, Newtown, Kilmainhamwood,
> collector P.J. Gaynor, 1941, NFC 792:101a-104a)

There are similar stories about a fairy doctor named Connor Sheridan living in Ballintogher, Gortloney, who died about 1870. His brother was also a priest who didn't approve of him.

Many years ago the then Parish Priest of Moynalty was going on foot to Brady's of Ballymacane [also called Canestown], and when passing by a well on the lands of a family named Flood, he heard a voice saying, 'All for me.' Just for a joke and not attaching any significance to the remark, he said, 'And some for me.' He did not see any person and did not bother looking for them. When he went to Brady's they made a complaint to him that they had little or no butter on their churn although they had a lot of cows at the time.

Next day his own housekeeper was churning; they had not much milk, but to her great surprise it wasn't long till the churn was full of butter. When she told the priest and showed him the butter he thought of the remark that he had heard when passing the well and what he had said as a joke in reply. He also recalled what the Bradys had told him about losing their butter, so he said some prayers, and after a short while the door opened and an old woman came in. She threw herself on her knees and said it was she was taking the butter. She promised never to do the like again, and she kept her promise.

(Collected by P.J. Gaynor in 1941 from Peter Rogers,
age 47, who heard the stories from John Rogers, who had
died twenty-five years previously, NFC 792:106a-108a)

Other methods mentioned elsewhere: add salt to milk, take the milk to the priest to have it blessed. A similar tale was told by A.H. Singleton:

Some years ago my brother bought a fine cow at a fair. When she was brought home I remarked that she had a piece of brown rag tied round her tail. I asked what it meant, and was told that it was to prevent her being 'overlooked', and the following 'true' story was related by way of illustration.

A man had a cow that was celebrated far and near for the quantity of milk she gave. Suddenly the supply stopped; the cow's milk had been 'taken' by somebody, but who could have done the deed? A rich but miserly neighbour was identified by the *pishogue* (i.e., wise woman) of the neighbourhood as having been the one to cast covetous eyes on the cow, and to transfer her milk to his own dairy. By the woman's advice a piece of his coat was surreptitiously procured and burned, the ashes carefully collected and tied round the cow's tail, when the charm was broken and her milk was restored to her.

… Some years ago there lived an old woman in the village of Drumconrath who was always sent for when the butter would not come. Our dispensary doctor told me that she used to walk three times round the churn *widdershin*, i.e., against the sun's course, muttering some incantation in Irish, after which there was no more difficulty about the churning.

(A.H. Singleton, 'Dairy Folklore and Other Notes from Meath
and Tipperary', *Folklore*, Vol. 15, No. 4, 1904)

A man at Herbertstown had his grain collected in the haggard and was troubled with rats and sent for the rat charmer. The charmer ordered all the rats out of the haggard and lined them up in the lane so he could send them off to the haggard of another farmer. They were all lined up and ready to go except one rat, which was still fumbling around in the haggard. The charmer ordered one of the rats to go back to the haggard and fetch the straggler. The rat went to the fence and got a stick and took it to the lone rat and put one end of it in its mouth. Then the two of them joined the rest. The straggler was blind.

'I heard that story twenty times,' James Caffrey, Jamestown, age 60, told collector D.F. O'Sullivan in 1938. (NFC 580:97)

30

HIDDEN TREASURE

There was a man one time and he lived near the moate of Kilbeg, near Kells in the County Meath. He left the country and went to Denmark where he got on well and prospered. One night he went to a spree, and in the course of the fun somebody asked him did he know anything about the moate of Kilbeg. He said he did – that he was reared beside it. They asked him if he heard of anything queer being ever seen around about it. He said that there used to be a black pig seen about it. They made up a sum of money for travelling expenses and gave him a knife and told him to go home and cut the tail off the black pig and bring it back to them.

He set out for home, and when he landed back he kept a watch around the moate and eventually saw the black pig. He seized the pig and cut off its tail and brought it back to Denmark. They fried it on a grisset [an iron pan with legs used to catch drippings from roasting meat], and when they had it fried they dipped their fingers in the grease and rubbed the grease to their eyes. They then looked into a mirror and said, 'It is there yet and will be for ever.'

When he got the chance he stuck his finger in the grease and rubbed it to his eyes, and when he looked into the mirror he saw the moate of Kilbeg and four or five big barrels of gold beside it. He began to cheer when he saw it, and someone asked him what was he cheering for. He told them that he saw four or five barrels of gold at the moate of Kilbeg. They asked him what eye did he see it with. He pointed towards one of his eyes, and a Dane stuck his finger in the eye and blinded it, saying, 'You will see no more of the gold.' But they had to make a collection and give him a big sum of money for the loss of his eye.

> (John Gargan, Dunarede, Kingscourt, heard that story from his father. Collector P.J. Gaynor, 1941, NFC 792:320-22)

A man dreamed that there was a crock of gold in the graveyard at Rathmore, and he got two friends to go with him one night to dig it up. They had a rule that no one was to say a wrong word or curse until they'd find it. They struck a flagstone, and one of them cursed. They unearthed two crocks, and when they uncovered them they found them full of sawdust. The charm had been broken.

They put the crocks back and headed home. They went back across the Deer Park at Rathmore out at Mooneystown or Garron and what did they walk into but six yeomen, so they got into difficulties then to get away from them. The yeomen wanted to know what they were doing, but they explained to them and told them all about what they were at, and they took their explanation and they got away safe. They might well have been arrested and got into further trouble, but they got away, and that ended the digging for the Crocks of Gold.

> (James Caffrey, Jamestown, aged 60, collector D.F. O'Sullivan, 1938, NFC 580:97)

John Caffrey lived in the shadow of Slieve na Cailligh. One evening he came across a leprechaun in a field near the house and managed to catch him and make him reveal the location of a crock of gold. John dug where the leprechaun directed him and found the gold, but it did him no good in the end. He fell ill and spent most of the money on cures, but died soon afterwards anyway. A large hump grew on his back, which they say killed him.

> (Collector/source W. O'Reilly, 1956, NFC 1440:93)

In AD 700, Danes landed between Mornington and Bettystown and sacked the monasteries and convents of Duleek. A young monk and other Irishmen escaped, taking with them all the gold, silver, manuscripts and other valuables, and buried them in a nearby bog. Just as they were returning from the bog, they were attacked by Danes and killed. It is not known which bog the treasure is buried in, and it is still there.

([Source name illegible] Corballis,
Duleek, 1938, NFCS 0682:206-207)

A man named Walsh from Keenogue took his family to America with a lot of money. When they arrived, he sent three pigeons back to Ireland, to Mr Loughran, who had moved into the house vacated by the Walshes. The first two pigeons arrived with the same message: 'There are riches and treasure in Keenogue Old House.' Unfortunately, the third pigeon lost the message he carried, and the treasure was never found.

(Seumas O Lochráin, aged 64, Caonóg, 1938, NFCS 0682:208-9)

In the ruined church in Rathmore, near Athboy:

In one of the half-dilapidated turrets is the sacristy (entered from the chancel), within which a heap of rubbish marks the operations of a treasure-seeker, who some years ago dreamed that the church plate and a sum of money were buried here in a corner. He came hither alone at midnight, and setting his lantern on the floor, commenced digging; but suddenly he heard an unearthly noise near the hearth, looked up, and saw, to his horror, the spectral form of a robed ecclesiastic frowning on him with a most threatening visage. The digger dropped his spade and fled, not daring to look behind till he reached the shelter of his own cabin. He never renewed his search, and his report sufficed to deter others from a similar attempt.

(Meath Antiquarian Society, *Rathmore and its Traditions*, 1880)

Many romantic stories of the treasure buried in these ruins were current a few years ago, and it is not long since hundreds of people, some of them from a considerable distance, assembled here by night, and made great excavations, in the hope of reaching the underground passage leading to the high altar, with the golden candlesticks, not to be touched under pain of death, by which lie two sleeping bishops, who, when awakened, will give the keys of two small chambers, one full of silver and the other full of gold, which may be taken away by the bold and pious finders. The police, however, who doubted the purpose of the assembly, interrupted the excavations, and the treasure was not disturbed.

(Richard Butler, *Trim Castle: Some Notices of the Castle and of the Ecclesiastical Buildings of Trim*, Dublin, 1861)

31

THE PROPHET MELDRUM

Meldrum, the prophet, who flourished about the beginning of the last [19th] century, was a servant boy with a priest at Kilmainhamwood. One morning he went to milk the priest's cow, and when returning with the can of milk it began to overflow. He drank some of it, and when he came home he told the priest what had occurred. The priest said, 'I wish you had waited till I drank it myself. You will be wiser in future than me.'

(Peter Rogers, 47, Newtown, Kilmainhamwood, collector P.J. Gaynor, 1941, NFC 792:117-118)

Another version told to P.J. Gaynor by his father, James, of Edengora, who died in 1926 aged 81, was that a bull came down out of the air and served a cow belonging to the priest, who told Meldrum to watch the cow when she was due to calve, and when she did calve to make sure that nobody drank any of the milk. The cow calved in due course and Meldrum drank some of the milk. When the priest heard that Meldrum had tasted the milk he said to him, 'You have what was intended for me.' After that Meldrum began foretelling future events.

[While the chapel at Lismeen Hill near Kilmainhamwood was being built] the prophet Meldrum came along and prophesied that

Mass would never be celebrated in it. The chapel was erected and the priest began to say Mass in it on the following Sunday. After the first gospel he thanked all who assisted in the building of the chapel, and said he, 'What about the fool, Meldrum, who said that Mass would never be celebrated here?'

Meldrum who was present, spoke up and said, 'Mass isn't finished yet. Do you not see the crack that is coming in the wall?'

The priest looked down and saw the crack in the wall; he and the congregation rushed from the building and it collapsed shortly after they had got outside. Meldrum's prophecy had come true.

(Peter Rogers, 47, Newtown, Kilmainhamwood, collector P.J. Gaynor, 1941, NFC 792:117-118)

32

HOLY
WELLS

Two English Baptists knocked on my door and informed me that they had been told by their ministers that Catholics worshipped the saints. I explained that the Catholic religion teaches us to worship only God; we are encouraged to *venerate* the saints as humans who served as models of how to live. No doubt some Catholics, not understanding the crucial difference between the words *worship* and *venerate*, would have agreed that they worship the saints. Do modern-day 'sun-worshippers' literally worship the sun as a god? I hope the Baptists went home and set their masters straight on the matter.

John M. Thunder, in 'The Holy Wells of Meath' in *The Journal of the Royal Historical and Archaeological Association of Ireland* (4:7, 1886-7), reflects this misunderstanding. Speaking of 'Well Worship', he says, 'We are assured that it was a prevalent superstition, and some who adored water as a propitious deity considered fire to be an evil one.'

Nearly 2,000 years ago, the Roman historian Tacitus understood the difference. He described the basis of the religion of the Celts thus: 'Their holy places are the woods and groves, and they call by the name of god that hidden presence which is seen only by the eye of reverence.'

Tacitus did not say the Celts *worshipped* trees. He said it was *among* the trees that they were more easily able to tune in to the presence of the supernatural. The same concept applies to holy wells: they're like outdoor churches. Similarly, during the phenomenon of the moving statues of Our Lady in the late 1980s, our parish priest plaintively expressed the hope that we would bring our devotion into the church, but he wisely chose not to denounce the gathering of the devout in front of the local statue.

Belying Thunder's use of the past tense for these 'superstitions', holy wells are still very much of the present. Comments such as 'Pilgrimages to holy wells was a feature of country life a century ago' and 'Until very recent times the custom of leaving votive offerings at holy wells survived' in *The Meath Chronicle* in 1957 suggest that some people don't get out enough. Visits to the reactivated St Kevin's Well in Glendalough peaked about five years ago, but return gifts for expected favours still decorate the nearby trees. One of the first of the returned 'disappeared' bodies was deposited by the PRIA next to the active St Brigid's Well at Faughart near Dundalk – the one at the top of the hill – under the neighbouring festooned hazel. The Well of Nemnach, the source of the River Gabhra, on the Hill of Tara was renovated recently and is popular with visitors.

> Local tradition says that three trout appear in Saint Kieran's Well in Carnaross the night before the pattern day, which is the first Sunday in autumn. They are called Faith, Hope and Charity, and their names are written on their backs. One man caught the fish and put them in a frying pan and started to cook them. One fish jumped out and said, 'Put us back where you got us,' which he did.
>
> (*Meath Holy Wells*, Noel French)

John Thunder also mentioned St Kieran's Well in his article:

> The branches of an ash spread over it, and it may be observed that a great number of our holy wells are shaded by this tree. The well was believed to contain several trout, each about a pound and a-half in weight; the people looked upon the fish with great veneration; and when it was necessary to remove them in order to clean the well, they were put back with scrupulous care. About the year 1840 a report was spread throughout Meath that the tree which shades St. Kieran's Well was bleeding; immediately the people for miles around flocked to the well, and brought with them bottles, that

they might carry home some portion of the precious fluid, their object being to use the blood as a cure!

Thunder's use of the exclamation mark there reveals his scepticism, as it does in his notice of St John's Well at Warrenstown: 'A popular belief is that the water – which is largely impregnated with iron – comes from the Jordan!' But his descriptions of these wells are neutral.

Tradition asserts that Columbkille, finding no water at Skryne, prayed that a spring might rise up; his prayer was heard, and, as a memorial of that event, he fixed iron nails in a flag-stone which is still visible at the well – having protuberances like the heads of nails.

About a mile from Syddan is the well of St. Biorran. It is said that a cripple was once carried on a litter to St. Biorran's Well, where he was cured, and able to walk home. He left behind him the litter, which took root, and a 'large tree grew from it'.

The well at Douth (Dowth) is called Tober Sencháin. A woman is reputed to have washed clothes in it, owing to which the well is said to have removed to a distance of nearly a mile to the south of the old church.

In 1939 for the Schools Collection, Patrick Smith, aged 84, Bolies, Duleek, explained the origin of St Cianán's Well at Keenogue. Cianán's mother was sick. There was no water in the house, and she asked Cianán to get her some. He thrust a stick into the ground right there, and a well sprang up next to his mother. She drank the water, and she was cured. (NFCS 0683:24)

The same series of articles in *The Meath Chronicle* that used the past tense regarding visits to holy wells produced this tale:

The legend of St. John's Well at Warrenstown, in the parish of Knockmark, recounts that John the Baptist was passing a rock in the Holy Land when he struck it with his staff, the point of which came out at Warrenstown, accompanied by a spring. People flocked to witness this wonder, bringing their ills, and some were cured.

33

NEWGRANGE – THE PALACE OF ANGUS

… a place of sacrifice used by the old Irish, and Mr. Cormuck O'Neil told me they had a vulgar legend about some strange operation at that town in the time of heathenisme …

(Molyneux, *A Discourse concerning the Danish Mounts, Forts and Towers in Ireland*, 1726)

Mounds and forts – any non-natural earthworks – were long attributed in the popular mind to a conflation of the Danes from Denmark with the Tuatha Dé Danann, the godlike race that mythological history says took possession of Ireland about 4,000 years ago. Chronicler George Story reported in 1691 that at the Siege of Limerick: 'The Danes encamp to the Left, where they found an Old Fort built by their Ancestors, which they were very proud of.'

During Professor Michael O'Kelly's excavation of the mound at Newgrange, the truth of that 'vulgar legend' was proved when he observed the midwinter sunrise shining into the chamber through the roofbox, the opening above the doorway, in 1969. It was only when he had cleared out the roofbox that the sun was able to enter the chamber for the first time in some 4,000 years. The sun reaches only to orthostat L19 through the doorway. That is the nineteenth stone on the left as you enter, decorated with a triple spiral.

'A tradition had long existed,' says Claire O'Kelly in her *Illustrated Guide to Newgrange*, 'that the rising sun, at some unspecified time, used to light up the 3-spiral stone in the end-chamber of the tomb.'

(It's in the end recess of the chamber, to be exact, and usually called the tri-spiral, as differentiated from the triple spirals on L19, the entrance stone and K52, the kerbstone diametrically opposite the entrance stone.)

The version I heard somewhere long ago was that there had been a local folk tale about Newgrange belonging to the sun god, and he visited his home once a year.

The poet-artist-mystic Æ (George Russell) heard or intuited or dreamed about that tradition. He published a short story in 1915 called 'A Dream of Angus Oge', in which Angus takes a young boy into the chamber of 'a great mound grown over with trees', which well describes Newgrange before excavation, and says, 'This was my palace.'

> And even as he spoke a light began to glow and to pervade the cave, and to obliterate the stone walls and the antique hieroglyphs engraven thereon, and to melt the earthen floor into itself like a fiery sun suddenly uprisen within the world, and there was everywhere a

wandering ecstasy of sound: light and sound were one; light had a
voice, and the music hung glittering in the air.

How did Æ know that the sun pervaded the chamber, when it wasn't
until more than fifty years later that the roofbox was cleared out and
sunlight was able to extend that far again?

In June 2001, the BBC conducted acoustic tests in the chamber for
a television programme, and in the days before Newgrange became a
superstar of tourist attractions various groups were allowed to perform
private rituals involving sound. There is a story that Æ and William
Butler Yeats visited Newgrange, and then or another time Æ fell asleep
at the mound. Did he have a vision of music hanging glittering in the
air when light and sound were one? I have a theory that could explain
Æ's description.

If you set a bucket or basin of water by a window where the
sun can strike it at a slant, and you stamp on the floor, the surface
of the water will jiggle, and the sun will throw dancing spirals
of light on the ceiling. If there was dancing or drumming in the
Newgrange chamber 5,000 years ago, with the basin in the end
recess filled with water and a flat reflective object behind it,
the sun entering through the roofbox would have struck the water
to create spirals dancing around the spiralled corbelled ceiling.
Unfortunately, the sun does not reach all the way to the back of
the recess nowadays. To test my theory, we have to wait another
21,000 years – the Great or Platonic Year is 26,000 years – for the
precession of the equinoxes to return the sun to the point where it
was when Newgrange was built.

A Second Chamber?

Visitors notice that the passage and chamber extend only one-third of
the way into the mound, and someone will invariably ask the guide
if there is another chamber. The guide often says 'no', but the correct
answer is that we don't know. With admirable restraint and humil-
ity, Professor O'Kelly left half of the mound unexcavated for future

archaeologists with more sophisticated methods. Probes into the mound around K52 opposite the entrance stone revealed no detectable spaces inside.

However, this brief notice appeared in the *Journal of the Royal Society of Antiquaries of Ireland* in 1893 from the distinguished antiquary and folklorist T.J. Westropp:

> Capt. Henry Keogh, R.M. of Tralee, writes to me stating that, on a visit to Newgrange, he discovered, between the right-hand recess and that facing the entrance, a passage, once closed by one of the great lining blocks of the central chamber. He says: 'I got my head and shoulders so far in that I was able to see that the passage turned towards the middle of the mound. It is nearly filled to the top with small broken stones and the parts of the large stones forming its sides are covered with carvings and spirals; it evidently leads to another chamber within the mound. Its exploration would probably result in an interesting discovery, and valuable arms and ornaments might be found.'

One of the retired guides told me that in the 1950s, Mr and Mrs Hickey used to guide people into Newgrange. One afternoon, they were sitting in front of the mound, when they heard a tremendous crash from within. They were afraid to go in alone, as it was getting dark and there was no electric light inside, so with reinforcements the following day they entered to see what had caused the noise. Nothing was out of place in the passage or the chamber. This incident, added to Captain Keogh's report, suggests that there may be an undiscovered passage and chamber.

The Spirit of Newgrange

Many of the guides you encounter at Newgrange, Tara, Trim Castle, Slieve na Caillí (Loughcrew) and Mellifont Abbey have been at the job for many years – they are rotated from place to place – and they are very knowledgeable and dedicated and extremely respectful of the sites. So incidents told to me by a couple of the guides surprised me, as much as they obviously spooked them.

In the Newgrange chamber, the guide usually stands with his or her back to the end recess, convenient to the light switch they use to recreate a pale imitation of the entrance of the sun. On a couple of occasions, the guide has felt a pressure from behind, as if a hand was trying to push them out of the chamber, and not in a particularly friendly manner.

Some people believe that the excavations in the 1960s and '70s ruined the character of the mound and destroyed its spirit. But others are not so sure.

The Souvenir Restored

There is a strong rule governing visits to any old place – stone circle, tomb, fairy fort, holy well or even a lone whitethorn tree in a field: leave a gift or token of respect if you wish, but never, ever take anything from it.

One of the official OPW guides at the Hill of Tara asked me one day if I had heard the news about the returned stone. No, I hadn't. She said that the Newgrange Visitors Centre had received a package from America. In the package was a stone, and with the stone was a note: 'Please return this stone to Newgrange. I took it as a souvenir, and I've had nothing but bad luck ever since.'

I asked Clare Tuffy, manager of the Boyne Valley complex that includes Newgrange and Tara, if the story was true. She said yes, and it wasn't the first time it had happened.

The Meaning of Newgrange

Many people have tried, with varying success, to interpret the enigmatic symbols carved in the stones. But symbols are the language of the subconscious, and those who built the passage tombs were human like ourselves. If we delve into our own subconscious and stretch our imagination, we might find some clues: what the symbols mean to us is probably close to what they meant to the builders.

On my first visit to Newgrange, Clare Tuffy had just started her job as a guide – 'baby-sitting a heap of rocks', as her friends joked – six months earlier, appropriately on the day of the winter solstice 1981. She was the only staff member present in the humble guide hut next to the mound. She had plenty of time to read a novel between infrequent visitors. Clare said that when she looked across the valley to the fields on the other side, she could imagine that the view would have been the same when Newgrange was built, minus a few houses. What Newgrange meant to her, she said, was continuity.

'Newgrange' is the name of the townland where the passage tomb known in the stories as Brú na Bóinne is located, and it is used as a short-cut for the proper term: the mound or passage tomb *at* Newgrange. The name comes from the new grange – an outlying farm – donated to the Cistercian monks at nearby Mellifont Abbey in 1142.

Chapter 34 tells some of the old stories of Newgrange under its original name of Brú na Bóinne.

THE RIVER BOYNE

A poet came to Fionn mac Cumhaill one day and challenged him to explain the meaning of two poems.

> I saw a house by a river's shore,
> Famed through Erin in days of yore,
> Radiant with sparkling gems all o'er,
> Its lord deep skilled in magical lore;
> No conqueror ever defiled its floor;
> No spoiler can rive its golden store;
> Fire cannot burn its battlements hoar;
> Safe it stands when the torrents pour;
> Feasting and joy for evermore,
> To all who enter its open door!
> Now if thou hast learned a champion's lore,
> Tell me the name of that mansion hoar,
> With roof of crystal and marble floor,
> The mansion I saw by the river's shore.

'I can explain that poem,' said Finn. 'The mansion you saw is Bruga of the Boyne, the fairy palace of Angus, the Dedannan prince, son of the Dagda, which is open to all who wish to partake of its feasts and its enjoyments. It cannot be burned by fire, or drowned by water, or spoiled by robbers, on account of the great power of its lord and master; for there is not now, and there never was, and there never shall be, in Erin, a man more skilled in magic arts than Angus of the Bruga.'

'That is the sense of my poem,' said the stranger; 'and now listen to this other, and explain it to me if thou canst.'

> I saw to the south a bright-faced queen,
> With couch of crystal and robe of green;
> A numerous offspring, sprightly and small,
> Plain through her skin you can see them all;
> Slowly she moves, and yet her speed
> Exceeds the pace of the swiftest steed!
> Now tell me the name of that wondrous queen,
> With her couch of crystal and robe of green.

'I understand the sense of that poem also,' said Finn. 'The queen you saw is the river Boyne, which flows by the south side of the palace of Bruga. Her couch of crystal is the sandy bed of the river; and her robe of green the grassy plain of Bregia, through which it flows. Her children, which you can see through her skin, are the speckled salmon, the lively, pretty trout, and all the other fish that swim in the clear water of the river. The river flows slowly indeed; but its waters traverse the whole world in seven years, which is more than the swiftest steed can do.'

(from *Old Celtic Romances* by P.W. Joyce, 1879)

How the Boyne Got its Name

This comes from the same conversation Cúchulainn had with his charioteer, Laeg, mentioned in chapter 17. When Emer asked him what route he travelled from Ulster to her house in Lusk in County Dublin, Cúchulainn used obscure names for the landmarks he traversed. Here he explains to Laeg the terms he used to describe crossing the Boyne:

'The road', I said, 'between the god and his Seer,' that is, between
Mac Oc of the Sid of the Brug [Oengus of Brú na Bóinne, ie,
Newgrange] and his seer. Bresal was a seer to the west of the Brug.
Between them was the one woman, the wife of the Smith. That is
the way I went. Mairne, then, is between the hill of the Sid of the
Brug in which Oengus is, and the Sid of Bresal, the druid.

'Over the Marrow of the Woman Fedelm,' I said, that is, the Boyne.
It is called Boyne from Boand, the wife of Nechtan, son of Labraid.
She went to guard the hidden well at the bottom of the dun with the
three cupbearers of Nechtan, Flex and Lesc and Luam. Nobody came
without blemish from that well, unless the three cupbearers went with
him. The queen went out of pride and overbearing to the well, and said
nothing would ruin her shape, nor put a blemish on her. She passed
left-hand-wise round the well to deride its power. Then three waves
broke over her, and smashed her two thighs and her right hand and
one of her eyes. She ran out of the Sid to escape from this injury until
she came to the sea. Wherever she ran, the well ran after her.

Segais was its name in the Sid, the river Segsa from the Sid to
the Pool of Mochua, the Arm of the Wife of Nuadu and the Thigh
of the Wife of Nuadu after that, the Boyne in Meath, Manchuing
Arcait it is called from the Finda to the Troma, the Marrow of the
Woman Fedelm from the Troma to the sea.

(From 'The Wooing of Emer', translated by Kuno Meyer, 1888)

Trinity Well, at the foot of Carbury Hill in County Kildare, is considered the source of the Boyne. Its old name is Tobar Segais, the same
Well of Wisdom where the Salmon of Wisdom lived before Finegas
caught it in a pool of the Boyne, Linn Feic, near Rosnaree, and Fionn
mac Cumhaill tasted it.

THE BOYNE AND THE BRÚ IN THE STORIES

Like the Hill of Tara, the Boyne is a setting for many of the great stories
of Ireland and for incidents in many more. Cúchulainn was born in
the Brú, making the Ulster hero a native of Meath. The tragic end of

Muirchertach mac Ercae (see chapter 8) was played out at Cletech on the Boyne and at the Brú. Cormac mac Airt died at Cletech and was buried at Rosnaree. Fionn mac Cumhaill died at Áth Brea on the Boyne, probably west of Slane (see chapter 21). Manannán mac Lir's boat, *Wave Sweeper*, which took its passengers anywhere the helmsman directed, was moored by an old mill at Áth na Bóinne at Rosnaree. In one of the Three Sorrowful Tales of Ireland, The Death of the Sons of Tuirenn, the three lads borrowed *Wave Sweeper* and set off from Rosnaree and returned there at the end of their adventures. In the Brú, the dead Gulbán was brought back to life in the form of a wild boar destined to kill Diarmuid and be killed by him in the story of the Pursuit of Diarmuid and Gráinne. On Diarmuid's death, Aonghus, his foster father, brought his body back to the Brú, where he was able to keep the soul connected with the body for three days so they could have a conversation.

The Brú is an entrance to the Otherworld, the interior a magnificent palace. It was the venue for the Feast of Manannán, which preserved the Tuatha Dé Danann from ageing, in which pigs that were eaten would come back to life on the following day; apples eaten sprouted on trees again. Curiously, a lot of what appeared to be pig bones were found near the entrance during excavation in the 1960s and '70s.

The name Brú na Bóinne, like the carvings on the stones, has stacked meaning. The word '*brú*' can be interpreted as 'womb' or 'river bank' or 'a place of accommodation', and all three senses apply to the womb of the goddess Bóann situated on the bank of the River Boyne that serves as a home, for a passage tomb is a symbol of the belly of a pregnant woman.

The Tuatha Dé Danann built the mounds we call passage tombs. They landed in the northwest, and so the mounds in Sligo are the oldest, dated to 4,000 BC and earlier. Those in the Boyne Valley, the most notable of which are Knowth, Dowth and the one best known as Newgrange, Brú na Bóinne, are the culmination of the tomb-builders' art and craft.

The Dagda Mór, the great good-at-everything god, whose names were Eochaid Ollathair (Horseman All-father) and Ruadh Rofessa (the Red Man of All Knowledge), was the chief of the Dananns. When they had finished building the mounds to live in, he selected

the best for himself. The problem was that it was already occupied by
Elcmar and his wife, Bóann. So he sent Elcmar on a task that should
have taken him one day, but as the sun god he had the power to stop
the sun for nine months. When Elcmar returned nine months later,
thinking he had been gone for one day, Bóann presented him with a
baby boy, saying, 'Isn't it wonderful: the child who was conceived in
the morning and born the evening of the same day.'

Of course, this was the Dagda's son Aonghus, who is the god of love
and of youth. The birds are his kisses. Manannán mac Lir did not like the
Dagda, and he taught Aonghus a trick to evict his father from the Brú.

When Aonghus had grown to young manhood, he asked the Dagda if
he could borrow the Brú for a day and a night. The Dagda reckoned that
since Aonghus was the god of love and youth he wanted to have a party
with his friends, and so he made himself scarce for a day and a night.

On his return he asked Aonghus to give the Brú back to him.
Aonghus refused, saying, 'You gave it to me forever.'

'No, I didn't,' said the Dagda. 'I gave it to you for a day and a night.'

'But all eternity is made of days and nights. Therefore you gave it
to me forever.'

In the face of such logical reasoning, the Dagda left and took up residence elsewhere, some say in the Donegal fort known as Grianán Ailigh.

So Aonghus still lives in the Brú, which is why it is also called
Caisleán Aonghusa – the Palace of Aonghus.

The Nurture of the Two Milk Vessels

Eithne, the daughter of the steward of the Brú, was insulted by a visitor
and refused to eat or drink anything but the milk of two cows imported
from India and milked by herself. Eventually, Manannán diagnosed
the problem. The insult had driven out her Danann spirit – her demon
spirit, by Christian interpretation – and it had been replaced by an
angel. This meant that she could no longer survive on the Otherworld
food that sustained the Tuatha Dé Danann. She lived by the Nurture of
the Two Milk Vessels for more than 2,000 years until St Patrick came
and baptised her. He tried to convert Aonghus but failed.

CÚCHULAINN REDDENS HIS WEAPONS

One day when Cúchulainn was 7 years old, he overheard Cathbad the druid tell his students that it was a good day for a boy to be given weapons for the first time. The boy who took arms that day, he said, would live a short but glorious life as a famous warrior, and his deeds would live after him.

Stretching the truth more than a little, Cú then went to his uncle, King Conor, and told him that Cathbad had said it was a good day for him to take arms. Conor believed him and gave him his own weapons, after the boy had broken all the others offered. Next on the agenda was the testing – reddening – of his new toys. On Cú's insistence, Conor's charioteer, Ibar, a brother of Laeg, who would be his charioteer for the rest of his career, took him on a tour of Ulster in Conor's own chariot. Ibar would soon swear it was the last time he'd take him anywhere. To cut an exhausting (for Ibar) itinerary short, they eventually arrived at Fincairn, the highest point on Slíab Moduirn (south of Castleblayney in County Monaghan) at 759ft, about 20 miles from home at Emain Macha.

Ibar pointed out sites of interest in Ulster and then the 'renowned places' in Meath, 30 miles to the south: Tara and Tailtiu, Cletech and Knowth and Brú na Bóinne and the fortress of the sons of Nechta Scene, which was just across the Boyne from the Brú.

'Are not these the sons of Nechta who boast that the number of Ulstermen alive is not greater than the number of those Ulstermen who have fallen at their hands?' asked the boy.

'They are indeed,' said Ibar.

'Let's go.'

'Whoever goes there, it won't be me.'

'You'll go alive or dead,' said the boy.

'Alive I shall go south,' sighed Ibar, 'but dead I know I shall be left at the stronghold of Nechta's sons.'

And so they went. There was a pillar stone in front of the fort with an iron ring and an ogam inscription: 'Whoever seeks combat should strike the pillar stone with the ring.' Cúchulainn uprooted the stone and threw it into the river.

Fóill son of Nechta got the message and soon arrived. Ibar warned Cú, 'No points nor weapons nor sharp edges harm him.' So Cú hurled an iron ball at him, and it took the ball's equivalent of his brains through the back of his head, and he was holed like a sieve so that the light of the air was visible through his head. And Cúchulainn struck off his head from his neck.

Fóill's brother Túachall arrived. 'Unless you get him with the first blow or the first cast or the first touch, you will never do so,' Ibar said. The boy threw Conor's spear at him, and it went through the shield and crashed through a rib on the far side after piercing his heart. Cúchulainn struck off his head before it reached the ground.

The youngest son of Nechta, Faindle, came. 'He travels over water like a swallow or squirrel. The swimmers of the world cannot cope with him,' Ibar warned. They met upon the water, and the boy clasped his arms around Faindle and held him until the water came up flush with him, and he dealt him a violent blow with Conor's sword and struck his head from his trunk, letting the body go with the current and taking with him the head. (Paraphrased with quotes from Cecile O'Rahilly's 1967 translation.)

THE POET AND THE SWAN

On a certain day the poet Mac Coisi was at the Boyne, where he perceived a flock of swans; whereupon he threw a stone at them, and it struck one of the swans on the wing. He quickly ran to catch it, and perceived that it was a woman. He inquired tidings from her, and what had happened unto her, and what it was that sent her thus forth. And she answered him: 'In sickness I was,' said she, 'and it appeared to my friends that I died, but really it was demons that spirited me away with them.' And the poet restored her to her people.

(From 'Of the Wonders of Ireland' in the Irish Nennius)

35

SLEEPING SOLDIERS

I heard tell of a man that lived a bit up from Rosnaree, and he was coming home from Drogheda and he was drunk staggering along the road when he saw a fort up a bit from Rosnaree Hill. Well, he stopped when he saw the light and a grand looking place on his left hand side and great light – the Boyne was on the right. Well, he walked into it and when he went in there were a lot of bags hanging around a big wall and there was a sword stuck in a bag. He went over and he was lifting up the sword and according as he was lifting it there was a man's head lifted up from this big bag and a horse along with him, and he was riding the horse, and as according as he drew out the sword there were horsemen rising all around the wall. They were nearly clear out of where they were and he got afeerd and he let the sword drop back in, and as soon as he did he was told, 'Go home, you coward.' I disremember the regiment he'd have lifted out of prison if he lifted up the sword altogether.

It is about 56 years since I heard an old man named Johnny Murray telling that. He'd be a man up to 70 years of age at that time. He used tell the story around the fire at night. He was a native of Rosnaree.

(James Neill, 74, Navan, collector
D.F. O'Sullivan, 1938, NFC 580:69)

In Meath, about fifteen miles from Ardee, there is a troop of cavalry enchanted in the Mote of Kilbeg. The spell can only be broken by firing a loaded gun which is in the cave. A man got in once and saw the troopers asleep in the saddle, with their faces on the horses' necks. He half-cocked the gun, and the soldiers at once sat half up, but he was afraid to do more and went away, leaving the gun on half-cock and the men sitting half up.

(From Jones in *Folklore*, 1908)

36

NAVAN

THE GHOST OF FRANCIS LEDWIDGE

> Kiss the maid and pass her round,
> Lips like hers were made for many.
> Our loves are far from us tonight,
> But these red lips are sweet as any.
> (First stanza of 'In a Café', Francis Ledwidge)

Matt McGoona, an old friend of the Slane poet Francis Ledwidge (1887–1917), was a printer at *The Meath Chronicle*. On 31 July 1917, he was working at the paper when he heard the familiar sound of Ledwidge's motorcycle outside. He was surprised, as he knew his friend was away at war on the Western Front with the British Army, and when he went outside to greet him, there he was in the clothes he normally wore when he was on the bike. But as he approached, Ledwidge suddenly disappeared. Matt learned a few days later that his friend had been killed in battle about the same time he saw his ghost in Navan.

The Meaning of Athlumney

Athlumney, from the Irish *áth luimnigh*, is the ford of 'a bare spot of land', according to John O'Donovan, but in the spirit of the Dindshenchas there is an alternative explanation, along with a story. This one derives the name from Áth Almaini, Ford of the Herds (*almach* [*alam*] 'having herds', eDIL). A keeper of a royal hostel looked after his herds so kindly that he didn't separate the cows from their calves. The cattle demonstrated their gratitude by gathering at the ford to mourn him when he died.

Or, stretching credibility a bit further, Áth Almaini could come from the overspill of a nearby tribe. According to John D'Alton in *The History of the County of Dublin* (1838), the *Book of Lecan* says that the maritime part of County Dublin north of the Liffey was called Almain and its inhabitants the Almanii. Might they have originally come from Germany (*Almain* = Germany, eDIL)?

The Burning of Athlumney Castle

Athlumney Castle is a fifteenth-century tower house to which a seventeenth-century mansion is attached. When its owner, Sir Launcelot Dowdall, a supporter of King James, heard that William had won the Battle of the Boyne in 1690, he burned his castle rather than see it fall into William's hands. That explanation of the destruction of the castle sounds more likely than the popular version that there were two sisters who were very competitive and envious of each other.

One owned Athlumney Castle, and the other owned Black Castle, just over a mile north on the other side of the Boyne. Following his attack on Drogheda in 1649, Cromwell was expected to come along the Boyne. The sisters agreed that, whichever of them first saw Cromwell's army approaching, she would set fire to her house to prevent its fall into the enemy's hands, and her sister would see the smoke and do the same to her house.

Cromwell didn't enter Navan by the main road from Slane (N51), which would have taken him past Black Castle, but turned off just before it at Donaghmore and crossed the Boyne over Babe's Bridge, if the story below is true. However, the owner of Black Castle set fire to a bundle of brushwood on the tower of her house anyway, knowing that her sister would take it as a signal to burn Athlumney, which she did.

BABE'S BRIDGE

James Grace reported in his sixteenth-century *Annales Hiberniae* that in 1330 there was 'a great flood, especially of the Boyne, by which all the bridges on that river, except Babe's, were carried away, and other mischief done at Trim and Drogheda.' (Not to be confused with Mabe's Bridge on the Blackwater north of Kells.)

A short walk along the Ramparts, the canal towpath on the Boyne, from Navan towards Slane will bring you to Babe's Bridge, with its single magnificent remaining arch of the original eleven standing in dignified isolation. It is the oldest stone bridge in Ireland. The fact that it was the sole survivor of the 1330 flood suggests that it was fairly new at the time, supporting a thirteenth-century dating based on the similarity of its architecture to that of St Michael's church in Duleek, which was built by Walter de Lacy in 1285, and its mention as a landmark in earlier thirteenth-century land grants. The design is unique in Ireland, though it has a near-twin in the intact fifteenth-century Pont Bohardy over the Èvre at Montrevault, which is still in use with a load limit of 1.5 tons. An internet search for 'Pont de Bohardy sur l'Èvre' will give you an idea of what Babe's looked like in its prime.

Babe's was a crossing point for the back road next to the Donaghmore church and round tower that runs between the race-course and the N51. The bridge was bequeathed 6 acres of land 'with the appurtenances' by John le Baub (or Balbie), hence the name, for the upkeep. Though it survived that 1330 flood, by 1463 'through default of repair, the said bridge is ruinous and like to fall speedily, unless it be now remedied' (Statute 3 Edw. IV c.82). Who would stoop so low as to steal from a cripple? Corrupt officials at Dublin

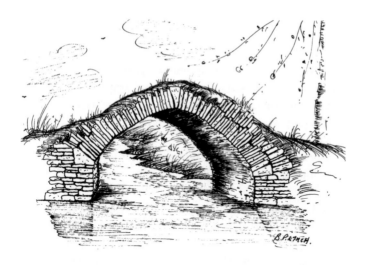

B. PRATCH.

Castle were pocketing Babe's income. By that same statute, Parliament 'ordained and agreed' that the custody of the bridge's property be given 'to the parson of Dunmoe and the vicar of Donaghmore for the time being, for the repair of said bridge, without interruption or hindrance of [the king] or his officers.'

Babe's continued to have an eventful life. According to local tradition, Cromwell's army crossed it on their way up the Boyne following the 1649 Siege of Drogheda. It acquired the nickname 'Robbers' Bridge' during the eighteenth century when horse thieves made it their hideout. But Hurricane Charley, nemesis of bridges all over Ireland, nearly destroyed it in 1986. Peter O'Keefe (*Irish Stone Bridges*, 1991) described the last surviving arch as 'a massively strong arch that would contain the thrust line of a locomotive within its middle third' – that is, the force exerted by a locomotive braking on the bridge – but when he inspected it after Charley he found that it was 'in imminent danger of collapse due to severe scouring of the abutment pier. The arch seemed to be no one's responsibility.'

The county engineer and the Office of Public Works came to the rescue and underpinned it, but history repeats: what happened to the income from those 6 acres and appurtenances?

TOM THE BUDDHA

'Buddha/Buddagh' comes from the Irish *bodach*, which is defined as 'churl, lout, beggar', but can be applied more positively to a person whose abilities belie his low social status. In Tom's case, 'Buddha' is probably also meant as a term of respect to acknowledge some degree of enlightenment.

This story was told by John Byrne to Colum Cromwell, who put it in his book, *Golden Wonders* (2001). Tom the Buddha, an illiterate local poet from Bohermeen, was sent to tell the priest he was needed to minister to a dying man.

As he rode his bike into the yard, Fr ___ was just arriving home from a day's huntin'. Before he dismounted, Tom shouted up his urgent message.

'Right, Tom,' says the priest, 'I'll be over in half an hour as soon as I get me dinner.'

Tom looked up at him and instantly proclaimed:

'At home in his bed lies a poor sinner.
His soul takes a chance while the priest eats his dinner.'

The following story about Tom was told to collector D.F. O'Sullivan in 1937 by Michael Manning, age 69, from Mooneystown, Athboy. (NFC 580:90)

I knew him well. He used be polishing the boys' boots in the seminary in Navan, and that is where he got his classical allusions. 'Buddagh' means a clown. He died in Trim in the county home about 1923.

He met two priests one time in Bohermeen at the Big Station who he was in the habit of knowing in the seminary, and one of them gave him a 1/- and Tom said, 'God bless you.' The other priest gave him 2/6, and Tom said, 'God Almighty bless you.' The first priest asked him the difference between 'God bless you' and 'God Almighty bless you'.

'Just eighteen pence,' he said.

Tom Smith was the Buddagh's name. He was very well known by all the clergy.

BARNEY CURLEY, MODERN FOLK HERO

'That day, the racegoers saw me as one of them and that was as important to me as winning the bet. ... I have always just wanted to beat the system.'

On 'that day' in 1987, Thoroughbred owner and trainer Barney Curley won £275,000 from a £126,000 stake, betting that he would saddle ten winners in three months. Friends jeered and bookmakers jumped at the offer, because Curley had had only nine winners in the previous two years. When the last of the ten hit the finish line in front within the time limit, the normally sedate Folkestone crowd cheered. 'I thought it was just me and the bookmakers in our own private war, until that tumult erupted,' Curley said.

'You can't beat the bookies' is good advice, but if everyone heeded it the bookies would soon be out of business. Curley believed he could ignore the advice, perhaps because when he briefly 'joined the enemy' but failed as a bookie he had been beaten himself. He bought a horse for £1,000 that he named Yellow Sam after his father's nickname. A poor runner in most track conditions – 'one of the worst horses I've ever owned' – he was an excellent jumper. There are many ways to improve a horse's chances of winning and many ways to improve a bettor's chances of scoring, and Curley used two that are legal.

First, he ran Yellow Sam against horses far above his class and in track conditions that showed him at his worst. That established a non-threatening form. Then he entered him against a poorer grade of competition in conditions that were ideal for him at Bellewstown on 26 June 1975, carrying the third lowest weight at 10st 6lb. The horse was priced at 20-1, logical odds given his track record. The problem was that Curley had a reputation as more than a bit of a chancer with a habit of winning, and if the bookies saw him placing a substantial sum on the horse, the odds would quickly plummet. So he meticulously planned the perfectly legal stroke that would make him famous far beyond racing circles. In his words, it was 'one of the biggest racehorse betting coups the world has ever known'.

He felt that Yellow Sam 'was capable of winning a bad race with everything going in his favour', so he chose Bellewstown, a minor track with a history dating to the eighteenth century, for two reasons: 1) the generally poor standard of the racing and in particular the amateur rider hurdle race he targeted, which he felt 'was probably worse than most races staged there'; and 2) the fact that there was only one public phone box on the course.

The latter was crucial. Nowadays you can place a guaranteed bet at, say, 12-1, and if the starting price (SP), the odds on the horse when the race starts, is less, you still get paid at 12-1. But at that time the shops would not guarantee a price, especially on one of Curley's horses, and bets were paid on the SP, so if Curley was to make a killing he had to make sure that the SP, which is determined by the on-course bookies, stayed high.

If anyone placed significant bets with the on-course bookies, they would lower the odds, so he sent a posse of friends and paid helpers to place bets of £50 to £300 in 150 shops around the country. Then he delegated a trusted confederate to monopolise the sole public phone on the course by pretending to be speaking with a terminally ill relative. The fictional call began twenty-five minutes before the start of the race and only finished at the off. Those in the queue could overhear one side of the emotional conversation and waited stoically. Besides natural sympathy for the supposed tragedy being played out, there were two reasons for their patience: the confederate was 'a tough sort that you wouldn't want to get into an argument with' who had the gift of the gab, and the first person in the queue was also a co-conspirator.

An hour and fifteen minutes before the off, Curley called some of his associates – the 'generals' – and told them to call the 'soldiers' in the shops fifteen minutes before the off to tell them to open the sealed envelopes they had been given and place the bet on the horse named inside. The reason for tying up the phone box was so that the off-course bookies couldn't contact their on-course colleagues to alert them to a suspected betting coup, which would have led them to lower the odds dramatically.

When a trainer is present at a race his horse is running in, bookies and bettors take that as a sign that the horse is expected to win, so Curley knew that if he was seen at Bellewstown on that day the odds would be affected. But he couldn't stay away, so he hid in gorse bushes in the centre of the track, entering surreptitiously from the back, to watch the action.

Curley had been down on his luck, and he invested his last £15,000 in the scheme. The horse won at 20-1 and netted him over £300,000, some €2 million in today's money. The bookies complained loudly, but they had to pay up. They did so grudgingly, forking over the entire amount in wadded-up £1 notes that reportedly filled 108 bags.

Curley could be forgiven for crowing: 'It was there to be done – and it worked.'

Yellow Sam won a race twelve days later at 5-2. Proceeds from Curley's autobiography, *Giving a Little Back* (1998), from which the above quotes were taken, go to Direct Aid for Africa. 'It's the safest bet there is,' Curley says. 'Give Him one good work, and He'll always give you back ten.'

38

MISCELLANEOUS TALES

Daniel O'Connell's 'Monster Meetings', which attracted 100,000 people regularly and half a million at the one at Tara on 15 August 1843, were so effective that the authorities banned one planned for Clontarf shortly after the Tara meeting. It was said that the meetings were advertised by the simple expedient of sending a wisp of straw from one person to another along with the message until the wisp and the news had reached everyone in the country. This story gives a variant of that method.

My mother, who died in 1917 at the age of 84 years, told me that when she was a little girl she saw people running with a stone from one house to the other and telling the people of that house that if they didn't leave the stone at the next house it would rise a plague and the family would be stricken with it. Later it was discovered what the whole thing really meant.

Dan O'Connell made a bet of £50 that he would 'warn all Ireland within twenty-four hours.' He got three stones and gave them to three men and told them to run to three houses and drop the stones there and tell the occupants that if they didn't run with the stones they would be stricken with a plague.

The plan worked so well and the people were so terrified by the idea of a plague that the three stones travelled to every house in the country within twenty-four hours, and O'Connell won his bet. My mother saw the people running from house to house with the stones. She said that all the world wouldn't put it out of her head the way that the people were running and the dread and fear that was on them. A man came running and left a stone at her father's house, and her brother took it and ran with it to the next house.

(Barney Gargan, Tierworker, collector
P.J. Gaynor, 1941, NFC 792:450-2)

This historical background will clarify the following story. Gormley was the daughter of Flann Sinna, high king 879–916. Flann killed Cormac mac Cuilennáin, king-bishop of Cashel, in battle in 908. It was Flann who commissioned the Cross of the Scriptures at Clonmacnoise, which depicts his ancestor Diarmait mac Cerbaill helping St Ciarán build the monastery.

Gormley married Cerball mac Muirecáin, an ally of her father's, who was killed in 909. Byrne (*Irish Kings and High Kings*) confirms that she 'had to endure his unseemly gloating and brutal insults after Cormac's defeat and death.'

Niall Glúndub (of the Black Knee) was a great-great-grandson of Niall Frossach (see chapter 4). He was high king on Flann's death in 916 until he was killed fighting the Dublin Norse in the Battle of Islandbridge in 919:

The Crawthee – the destroyed house – is at the Hill of Ward outside Ballyboy townland near the town of Athboy. The story goes that Niall of the Black Knee lived there and Gormley the daughter of the king of Meath was betrothed to King Cormac and went with her train and suit for to be married and had to return as Cormac had taken a vow of celibacy. There was a battle fought between her father's army and Cormac's army in Munster as he didn't accept her in marriage.

She afterwards married a king of Leinster and her husband went
to boast on his return home after beating Cormac in battle and
there came friction between them and she called him a coward and
he struck her and she was separated from him and after he died
she was married to Niall of the Black Knee or Niall na glun dubh.
I think she was the only daughter of the King. I can't think of his
name now. He was descended from the Milesians.

The Mansion was thatched with the feathers of the wild birds of
the forest and there were 24 rooms in it and all in beehive shape.

The Munster men on one of their forays burned the Royal
Mansion under the Hill of Ward-Clachta. It is also the right name
of Athboy (Athbwee na clachta).

(Michael Manning, Mooneystown, Athboy, aged 70, 1938,
collector D.F. O'Sullivan, NFC 580:62)

Jemmy the Huntsman followed the Meath Hunt dressed in cast-
off white breeches and a faded red coat some sizes too big, with a
strong rope tied across his shoulders and a few towels, ready to pull
any sportsman out of a bog hole or river and give them a wipe over
and dry the saddle. The fee was never less than half a crown.

When [George] Wyndham was Chief Secretary for Ireland [1900–
1905], he was fond of taking a day off and having a gallop with the
Meath Hounds. By all accounts he was not a great horseman nor
was he over-strong. One frosty, chilly morning he was negotiating a
river with boggy sides. The horse dropped his hind legs and shifted
Wyndham on to the soft mud. Jemmy the Huntsman, having a well-
trained eye, suspected an odd casualty at this fence and was not long
in coming to the help of the Chief Secretary. Jemmy caught the horse
and put the Chief Secretary on dry ground and commenced to clean
him down, and then gave him a leg up on to the saddle. As soon as
the Chief Secretary was safely mounted, he put his hand in his pocket
and produced six pence in silver and handed it to Jemmy.

Jemmy looked at it in the palm of his hand, took off his battered
hat and proceeded to curse Kruger. [Paul Kruger was the President

of the South African Republic who declared war on Britain in 1899. The Second Boer War continued until 1902.]

The Chief Secretary looked at him in wonder, saying, 'I thought all Irishmen were in favour of the Boers. Why then should you curse Kruger, who is their leader?'

'He did me a very bad turn in my profession,' replied Jemmy.

'Why and how?' retorted the Chief Secretary.

'Because,' said Jemmy, 'he killed all the half-crown men and only left me the six-penny ones.'

(Collector/source W. O'Reilly, 1956, NFC 1440:36-7)

In my father's young days a number of men were planting trees on a moate in the townland of Balgree, in the parish of Kilskyre and Ballinlough. One man was trying to remove a stone with a crow-bar, and when he got the stone shifted the crow-bar slipped and went away down in a hole in the moate. They could hear it rattling as it went down, and it took it a while to get to the bottom.

(Daniel Lynch, 69, Tullyatten, Mullagh, heard stories from his parents, who were natives of Moynalty parish, collector P.J. Gaynor, 1941, NFC 792:265-6)

A man lived alone in Dromone next to Slieve na Cailligh. He had a sister who was committed to the asylum in Mullingar. She asked him to bury her in Moylagh when she died, and he promised that he would, but she was buried in Mullingar before her brother learned of her death. Some nights later, she appeared to him and asked him to fulfil his promise, but he didn't. A few nights later she pulled him out of bed, so the following night he and a companion went to the graveyard in Mullingar and dug up a grave, but discovered it was the wrong one. Eventually they found the right one and dug her up and buried her in Moylagh, and nothing more was heard from her.

(Collector/source W. O'Reilly, 1956, NFC 1440:94-5)

It is believed by many people in this district (Oldbridge) that most of Mr Coddington's fields are enchanted. There is one field along the river and on Hallow Eve little red men are supposed to have been seen dancing in it.

On this night many years ago there was an old man walking home across this field when he saw these little red men playing football. They stopped playing when they saw the old man coming and ran up to him and asked him to kick their football. He did so, and kicked it so far that it disappeared out of their sights. They were very cross when they saw what he had done, and they flew at him in a rage and beat him until he was nearly dead. Then they disappeared.

(Patrick McGuinness, 50, Oldbridge, Drogheda, told this story to his daughter, Peggie, in 1938, NFCS 0682:6)

A man, who resided in a house adjacent to [an old castle in the townland of Carrickdexter about 3km west of Slane], shortly after it was deserted, had the honour of breakfasting one morning together with a very little old man, who came into his house a few minutes before breakfast. After his repast he took up his leg and put it in such a position as to rest his head on the sole of his foot, or rather on his big toe which was as broad as the palm of any Meathian's hand.

(John O'Donovan, *Ordnance Survey Letters Meath*, 1836)

The fourteenth- or fifteenth-century bell tower known as the Yellow Steeple is all that remains of the thirteenth-century Augustinian abbey of St Mary in Trim, founded by St Patrick and allegedly destroyed by Cromwell. The abbey became famous for the statue of Our Lady, installed about 1370, to which were attributed many miracles. The *Annals of the Four Masters* enumerate a few:

1397: 'Hugh Mac Mahon recovered his sight by fasting in honour of the Holy Cross of Raphoe, and of the image of the Blessed Virgin Mary at Ath-Trim.'

1412: 'The Image of the Blessed Virgin Mary of Ath-Trim wrought many miracles.'

1444: 'A great miracle was wrought by the image of the Blessed Virgin Mary at Trim, namely, it restored sight to a blind man, speech to a dumb man, and the use of his feet to a cripple, stretched out the hand of a person to whose side it had been fastened, *et foeminam gravidatam feles eniti fecit* [and it made a pregnant woman give birth to cats].'

So popular was the shrine that the government extended protection to 'rebels' so they could visit it without fear of official harassment. An Act of Parliament in 1472 (12 Edw. IV c.20) provided the means for the establishment and maintenance 'and perpetual continuance of a perpetual wax candle from day to day and night to night burning before the image of our Blessed Lady' and for the installation and maintenance of an additional four wax candles to burn before the image during Masses and devotional services in her honour 'for the good estate of [King Edward IV] and Cecilia his mother, and of his children, and for the souls of their progenitors and ancestors.'

Alas, that 'perpetual continuance' came to an end in 1538 when the Protestants 'burned the images, shrines, and relics, of the saints of Ireland and England; they likewise burned the celebrated image of the Blessed Virgin Mary at Trim, which used to perform wonders and miracles, which used to heal the blind, the deaf, and the crippled, and persons affected with all kinds of diseases; and they also burned the staff of Jesus, which was in Dublin, performing miracles, from the time of St. Patrick down to that time, and had been in the hands of Christ while he was among men' (AFM at 1537).

❧

They bribed the flock, they bribed the son,
To sell the priest and rob the sire;
Their dogs were taught alike to run
Upon the scent of wolf and friar.
(From 'The Penal Days', Thomas Davis)

In the Penal Times around the turn of the eighteenth century, a 'reward' or bribe of £5 or £10 was paid for information leading to the capture of an unregistered priest. A similar bounty on wolves about the same time drove them to extinction. Priest-hunters were particularly hated by the people. Father John O'Hanlon, author of the encyclopaedic nine-volume *Lives of the Irish Saints* (1873 *et seq.*), points out in *Legend Lays of Ireland* (1870) that laws were passed in the early eighteenth century whereby,

if an unregistered priest were detected, a heavy fine was imposed on the Papists – as they were insultingly termed – of the county where he was discovered, and the proceeds were directed to be paid as a reward for the informer. This provision soon created a miscreant class of detectives, usually denominated 'priest-hunters', who obtained fifty pounds per head for the discovery of an archbishop, a bishop or an ecclesiastical superior, and twenty pounds were given for the prosecution of other ecclesiastics. … In several instances, the gentry and magistrates, through prejudiced and bigoted motives or through a misguided opinion of official duty, joined in the pursuit of priests.

❧

At that time there was a landlord and priest-hunter named Peters, for whom Petersville is named. He had a workman who was a non-practising Catholic, and Peters thought he'd use him as bait to kill a priest who he heard was hiding at Newtown near Kilmainhamwood. He told the healthy workman to get into bed and pretend he was sick, and then he sent word to the priest that his presence was required to administer the Last Rites.

Peters had a gun ready to shoot the priest while he performed his function, but when the priest saw the man in the bed he said, 'The man is dead already. It's too late now.'

When Peters saw that the man was really dead, he got such a fright that he let the priest go and never bothered him again.

Some local men knocked on the door of the pub in Kilmainhamwood at 7.20 one morning looking for drink and woke up the barman, George McCormack, who was sleeping upstairs. He told them he wouldn't open the pub until he heard the Angelus bell ring. One of the men, Bill Cruise, rose to the challenge. He managed to get the key to the church and went in and rang the bell. True to his word, George came down and opened up. (Story from Jack McKenna in *Kilmainham of the Woody Hollow* by Danny Cusack.)

[My mother recalls] the day that granddad was on his way out the front door to go to the bank … when granny admonished him for wearing his old dungarees. My mother never forgot by way of defence his response: 'Maggie, those who know me know I have better, and those who don't know me don't give a damn!'

(Louise Scott in *Meath Voices* by Tommy Murray)

Pat Martin, a farmer aged about 60 in 1938, said that Moyaugher means 'The Plain of the Slaughtered Horses'. This was O'Farrell country, and a troop of Talbots invaded about the year 1120 and ordered their fighters to kill their own horses so that they could not retreat.

(Pat Martin, 60, Jamestown, 1938,
collector D.F. O'Sullivan, NFC 580:93)

I particularly enjoyed this yarn from Michael Gaffney, Relaghbeg, Mullagh, Kells, who heard stories from his father and grandfather sixty years before he told them to collector P.J. Gaynor in 1941 (NFC 792:259-61). I heard it at summer camp in Michigan when I was 10 years old, which doesn't necessarily mean that it didn't happen in Meath:

> There was a fellow one time and he was afraid of nothing. One night some friends of his made a bet with him that he wouldn't go into a vault and drive a nail into one of the coffins. They were to remain outside the vault so that they could hear him driving the nail. He went into the vault, and they could hear him driving the nail, but he didn't come out again. When they despaired of him coming out they lit a light and went into the vault. And when they went in they found him dead and the tail of his coat nailed to the coffin. He had put the nail through his coat in the dark, and when he started to move away found himself held back, and the fright killed him.

Many years ago a family named McEntee resided at Ballymacane. They were big landowners, and they used to make poteen. Every night that they had on 'a brew' their women would be watching for the gaugers. One night while the men were making a brew the door opened and an old woman came in. She walked over to the fire; sat down beside it, and almost immediately disappeared. They then saw on the chair where she had been sitting a bunch of blue-bells similar to those growing on a grave in a fort at Mullanasthohan. The McEntees took this as a warning that the gaugers were coming.

They cleaned away everything connected with the brew, and in a few minutes the gaugers arrived but found nothing.

> (Peter Rogers, 47, Newtown, Kilmainhamwood,
> collector P.J. Gaynor, 1941, NFC 792:115-116)

There are many anecdotes in the Drogheda area about the Robin Hood-like Michael Collier (1780–1849), known as Collier the Robber. Here is one:

One night he came to a cottage in the country and he asked the woman of the house if she would give him shelter until morning. During the night the woman told him that she would have to leave the house in the morning as she had no money to pay the rent. Collier gave the woman £5, so when the landlord came next morning she gave him the rent. No sooner had the man gone when Collier followed him and robbed him of the money, which he gave back to the poor woman.

> (Mrs O'Toole, aged about 56, Donore, Drogheda,
> collected by Frances O'Toole, 1938, NFCS 0682:9)

There was a priest in this district named Father Cullen. One morning during the Famine he was going around begging food for the poor and he came to the house of a Catholic and asked him in God's name to give him some food for the poor, but the man said he couldn't afford it. When the priest was returning he met the man again, and this time he asked the priest what prayers he prayed on him as all his potatoes had gone bad. The priest said that he didn't pray any prayers on him, but when he refused to give the potatoes to the poor he refused them to God.

> (John Bates, aged 74, Sheephouse, Drogheda,
> collector Patrick Lennon, 1938, NFCS 0682:88)

A man was cutting a tree one time, and he stopped to get his dinner, and when he came back it was standing as before as thick as four trees, and no mark of the saw in it. Nobody ever took a stick out of it, because Thomas Heaney brought home a log out of it one night, and just put it on the fire. There was no fire in the grate at the time, and it burned away.

(Tommy Heaney, aged 70-80, Garballagh, Duleek,
collector Rónán Ó Braonán, NFCS 0682:228)

❧

A group of men used to play cards in a field near the church on Sundays instead of attending Mass. One day the priest came to them and asked them why they weren't at Mass. No sooner were the words out of his mouth than the cards went up in flames. The men never missed a Sunday Mass after that.

A man used to plough on Sundays. One Sunday when he was ploughing the ground opened up and swallowed him.

(Patrick White, Duleek, NFCS 0683:32)

❧

Long ago a man built a shop in Duleek, stocked it well, and opened it on a Wednesday. He neglected to put out the fire when he closed that night, and a mat in front of the fireplace caught fire and burned the shop down. Another man opened a business in the same street on a Thursday, and it was also destroyed. That is why, they say, people in Duleek reckon that Friday is the best day to embark on an enterprise.

(NFCS 0683:56)

❧

The Big Wind of 6 January 1839, a Category 3 hurricane with the extremely low pressure of 918 hectopascals, left several hundred dead, severe property damage and forty-two ships reported wrecked. Some say it was the exodus of the fairies that caused it.

❧

An old woman named Frances McGowan lived in a thatched house in Corballis. She was always worried that sparks from the chimney would set the thatch on fire. A neighbour, Josie Mansfield, told her about a dream she had.

'There was a big wind, and your house caught on fire. You came running out calling for help. Then you reached under a big stone and pulled out a big cross. You turned the stone and lifted the cross, and then you went back to your house and threw water on the fire to prevent the sparks from reaching the roof, and then the fire went out.'

A few nights later, the famous Big Wind struck Ireland. Events happened just as Josie had foretold. The house went on fire. Frances went out and found the stone and cross, threw water on the fire and quenched it.

(Nicholas Connell, Longford, Duleek, NFCS 0683:83-4)

St Patrick established a bishopric at Duleek and installed St Cianán as bishop. Cianán (d. 489) built the first stone church in Ireland, hence the name of the town, 'stone church', from the Old Irish *dáim liacc .i. tegduis cloch* (eDIL); previous churches had been built of wattle. This story about Cianán as a child was told by Risteard Ó Concubhair, aged 76, Commons, Duleek, to his grandson, Seán Ó Concubhair in 1938 (NFCS 0682:227).

The family were going to Mass, and they told Cianán to stay home and keep the crows from eating the seeds of the wheat that had been planted. But Cianán wanted to go to Mass, so he gathered all the crows and shut them up in the barn and set off for the church. When the family saw him, they berated him for neglecting his duty, but when they got home he opened the barn doors, and out came all the crows.

There is a large building at the mouth of the River Boyne called the Maiden Tower. The top of it is battlemented and it is 80ft in height. The tower might have been used to carry a beacon for the ships coming

into the river on their way to Drogheda. There are two stories in connection with it. One is that there was once a lady whose husband was
a soldier. One day he was called away to the war. He told her that if he
returned dead they would hoist a black flag and if alive a white one.

When the day came on which he was about to return the lady
went up on the tower to see the boat return. At last it came near
and the soldier was safe, but for a joke the sailors hoisted a black
flag. The lady seeing it jumped from the tower and broke her finger.
That is why the other little building is there. It is called the Lady's
Finger. It is 17ft high. Both are in an excellent state of preservation.

Alternatively, she was killed when she fell.

(Peter Connolly, 69, Mornington, told this story to Lilly Connolly
in 1938, NFCS 0682:170)

Ann Kelly, 69, Mornington, added that the husband built 'The Lady's
Finger' in her memory. (Collected by Peggy Bradigan in 1938,
NFCS 0682:171.)

There is another story in connection with the Tower. There was
once a girl put out of her home. She was sitting on some stones
sewing, and she wished that she had some place to shelter for the
night. While she was asleep the tower sprung up over her.

(John Barret, 73, Bettystown, 1938, collector John Taylor
NFCS, 0682:159)

William Wilde in *Beauties of the Boyne* (1849) adds: 'Not many years ago a poor half-witted female recluse took up her abode on the top of the tower, and was, like the hermits of old, supplied with every necessary by the surrounding peasantry. It has been conjectured that the tower was erected during the reign of Elizabeth, and took its name from the Maiden Queen.'

It was originally called Mayden Tower, from Maydenhayes, the name of the locality.

> By Nanny Water where the salty mists
> Weep o'er Riángabra let me stand deep
> Beside my father.
> (From 'The Death of Leag, Cuchulain's Charioteer', Francis Ledwidge)

Laytown – Laig Dún – is named for the mound north of the River Nanny called the Moate, where Laeg son of Riángabra, Cúchulainn's charioteer, is buried. A local man is the subject of a version of the 'Monday, Tuesday' tale of two hunchbacks, one having his hump removed for his kindness to the fairies, and the other given the first one's hump for his disrespect. The Moate is said to represent the double hump of the second man. (Bridget Taylor, aged 65, Bettystown, Drogheda, collector John Taylor, 1938, NFCS 0682:162-3.)

Black and Tans stationed at Whitewood House near Nobber got a fright when they saw a light coming from Whitewood Lake. They challenged it twice with no response. Then they fired several volleys at it, but it kept coming at them. They ran into the house and fired Vesey lights. The Tans in Kells saw the lights but did not come until daylight. Bullets from the volleys were found on the far side of the lake. 'There was always "something" about Whitewood Lake,' concluded Daniel Lynch, 69, Leitrim, Mullagh, Moynalty, when he told the story to collector P.J. Gaynor in 1942 (NFC 830:21).

BIBLIOGRAPHY

BOOKS AND ARTICLES

Annales Hiberniae, attributed to James Grace, fifteenth century

Annals of the Four Masters (in full: *Annals of the Kingdom of Ireland from the Earliest Times to the Year 1616*) – see O'Donovan, John

Bhreathnach, Edel (ed.), *The Kingship and Landscape of Tara* (Four Courts, 2005)

Brennan, Conor, *Yellow Furze Memories* (1996?)

Butler, Richard, *Trim Castle (Some Notices of the Castle and of the Ecclesiastical Buildings of Trim)* (Dublin, 1861)

Byrne, Francis J., *Irish Kings and High Kings* (Batsford, 1973; Four Courts, 2001)

Byrne, Patrick, *Irish Ghost Stories* (Mercier, 2000)

Campbell-Kease, John (ed.), *Tribute to an Armorist, Essays for John Brooke-Little* (The Heraldry Society; London, 2000)

Campion, Edmund, *A Historie of Ireland* (1571)

Colgan, John, *Trias Thaumaturga: The Three Wonderworking Patrons of Ireland* (1647)

Condit, Tom, 'Travelling Earthwork Arrives at Tara', *Archaeology Ireland*, Vol. 7, No. 4, Winter 1993

Conwell, E.A., *Discovery of the Tomb of Ollamh Fodhla* (1873)

Corcoran, J. Aeneas, *Irish Ghosts* (Geddes & Grosset; New Lanark, Scotland, 2002)

Cromwell, Colum, *Golden Wonders* (2001)

Curley, Barney, *Giving a Little Back* (Collins Willow; London, 1998)

Curran, Bob, *A Haunted Land* (O'Brien Press; Dublin, 2004)

Cusack, Danny, *Kilmainham of the Woody Hollow, a History of Kilmainhamwood* (Kilmainhamwood Parish Council, 1998)

D'Alton, John, *The History of the County of Dublin* (1838)

Dictionary of the Irish Language, E.G. Quin *et al.* (eds), (Royal Irish Academy, Dublin 1913-76). The version consulted was the 2007 online edition, eDIL (www.DIL.ie).

Doyle, Eamon, *The Wexford Insurgents of '98 and Their March into Meath* (Duffrey Press; Enniscorthy, 1998)

eDIL – see *Dictionary of the Irish Language*

Elizabeth, Countess of Fingall, *Seventy Years Young* (Collins; London, 1937; Lilliput Press; Dublin, 1991)

Ellis, Peter Berresford, *The Boyne Water: the Battle of the Boyne* (Blackstaff, 1989)

French, Noel, *Meath Holy Wells* (Meath Heritage Centre; Trim, 2012)

Ginnell, Laurence, *The Brehon Laws: A Legal Handbook* (1894)

Gormanston, Eileen (Eileen Butler Preston), *A Little Kept* (Sheed and Ward; London, 1953)

Gwynn, Edward, *The Metrical Dindshenchas* (School of Celtic Studies, Dublin Institute for Advanced Studies, 1903, 1906, 1935). Available online at CELT (Corpus of Electronic Texts).

Hickey, Elizabeth, *I Send my Love Along the Boyne* (Dublin, 1966; Drogheda, 2000)

Hollo, Kaarina, 'Cú Chulainn and Síd Truim', Ériu 49 (1998)

Hore, Herbert Francis, 'The Ossianic Age', *Ulster Journal of Archaeology*, VI (1858)

Irish Nennius: *The Irish Version of the Historia Britonum of Nennius*, the eleventh-century translation into Irish of the ninth-century *Historia Brittonum*, ed. and trans. (James Henthorn Todd; Dublin, 1848)

Jones, Bryan H., 'Irish Folklore from Cavan, Meath, Kerry, and Limerick', *Folklore*, Vol. 19, No. 3 (1908)

Keating, Geoffrey, *History of Ireland* (1634)

Kelly, Fergus, *Audacht Morainn* (The Testament of Morann) (Dublin Institute for Advanced Studies, 1976)

Lover, Samuel, *Legends and Stories of Ireland* (1831, 1834)

MacManus, Seumas, *The Story of the Irish Race* (USA, 1921)

Martin, P., 'The Oldcastle Speaking Stones', *The Breifny Antiquarian Society Journal*, I, II (1921)

Martyrology of Oengus – ninth-century accounts of saints and their feast days

Meath Antiquarian Society, *Rathmore and its Traditions* (1880)

Molyneux, Thomas, *A Discourse concerning the Danish Mounts, Forts and Towers in Ireland* (1726)

Moore, Beryl, 'Exploring Clonabreany', *Ríocht na Midhe*, III, 3 (1965)

Morrissey, James F. (ed.), *Statute Rolls of the Parliament of Ireland*, Vol. IV (Stationery Office; Dublin, 1939)

Murray, Tommy, *Meath Voices* (Tempus/Nonsuch, 2006)

Nolan, Pierce Laurence Mary, 'The Month of Mary: Our Lady of Trim', *Ave Maria* (*c*. 1894)

Ó Súilleabháin, Seán, *Miraculous Plenty: Irish Religious Folktales and Legends* (Four Courts; Dublin, 2012); English translation of *Scéalta Cráibhtheacha* (1952)

O'Curry, Eugene, *Manners and Customs of the Ancient Irish* (1873)

O'Donovan, John, *Annals of the Four Masters* (in full: *Annals of the Kingdom of Ireland from the Earliest Times to the Year 1616*)

O'Donovan, John, *Ordnance Survey Letters Meath* (1836)

O'Hanlon, John, *Legend Lays of Ireland* (Dublin, 1870)

O'Hanlon, John, *Lives of the Irish Saints* (London, New York, 1873 *et seq.*)

O'Hanlon, John, *The Buried Lady: A Legend of Kilronan* (Dublin, 1877)

O'Keefe, Peter, *Irish Stone Bridges: History and Heritage* (Irish Academic Press, 1991)

O'Keeffe, John, *Recollections of the Life of John O'Keeffe* (Coburn; London, 1826)

O'Kelly, Claire, *Illustrated Guide to Newgrange and the Other Boyne Monuments* (1978)

O'Rahilly, Cecile, *Táin Bó Cuailnge from the Book of Leinster* (Dublin Institute for Advanced Studies, 1967)

Petrie, George, *The Round Towers of Ireland: the Ecclesiastical Architecture of Ireland* (1845)

Plummer, Charles, *Lives of Irish Saints* (Oxford, 1922)

Radner, J.N., 'The significance of the threefold death in Celtic tradition', *Celtic Folklore and Christianity*, Patrick K. Ford (ed.), (McNally and Loftin, Santa Barbara, USA, 1983)

Ryan, John, 'The Abbatial Succession at Clonmacnois', *Féilsgríbhinn Eóin mhic Néill*, John Ryan (ed.) (Dublin, 1940)

Singleton, A.H., 'Dairy Folklore and Other Notes from Meath and Tipperary', *Folklore*, Vol. 15, No. 4 (1904)

Statute Rolls – see Morrissey, James F.

Stokes, Whitley, 'The Prose Tales in the Rennes Dindshenchas', *Revue Celtique*, 16 (1895)

Story, George, *A true and impartial history of the most material occurrences in the kingdom of Ireland during the last two years* (London, 1691)

Trench, C.E.F., *Slane* (An Taisce; Slane, 1976, 1987)

Wakeman, William F., *Handbook of Irish Antiquities* (1891)

Walsh, Paul, *Leaves of History*, Series I, (Drogheda, 1930)

Walsh, William J. (ed.), *The Apparitions and Shrines of Heaven's Bright Queen in Legend, Poetry and History*, Vol. 1, Carey (New York; Burns & Oates, London, 1904)

Wilde, William R., *The Beauties of the Boyne and its Tributary the Blackwater* (Three Candles; Dublin, 1949) (original edition 1849)

Wood-Martin, W.G., *The Lake Dwellings of Ireland* (Dublin; London, 1886)

ORAL SOURCES

Leonard Barber
Richard Barber
T.P. Callaghan
Charlie Clarke
Shelia Clarke
Kathleen Cooney
Al Cowan
Danny Cusack
Patricia Donnelly
Philip Donnelly
Joe Gargan

Marion Gilsenan
Malachy Hand
Mickey Kenny
Teddy McCabe
Hughie McCusker
Ciaran McDonald
John McDonnell
Eileen O'Reilly
Hugh O'Reilly
Kevin O'Reilly
Catherine Stafford

ACKNOWLEDGEMENTS

I am grateful for the resources and the generous help of the staff at the National Library of Ireland, the National Folklore Collection at University College Dublin, the Royal Society of Antiquities of Ireland, and the Meath County Library. Also, *Ríocht na Midhe* and the Meath authors of locally published and self-published books, especially the prolific Tommy Murray, where I have found some of these stories, deserve credit for collecting and disseminating their heritage.

ILLUSTRATIONS

Sarah Carney: 'Tri-spiral Newgrange', p. 152

Hugh O'Connor: 'Cormac Blinded', p. 62; 'Death of Fionn', p. 112

Fiona Dowling: 'Werewolves', p. 76

Lisa Lennon: 'Headless Man', p. 33

Brendan Lynch: 'Cross of the Scriptures', p. 57; 'Market Cross Kells', p. 71; 'Tower of Lloyd Kells', p. 73; 'Newgrange exterior', p. 156; 'Babe's Bridge', p. 169; 'Yellow Steeple Trim', p. 179; 'Maiden Tower and Lady's Finger', p. 186

Carmen Merina: 'Daniel O'Connell', p. 79

Eléonore Nicolas: 'Gormanston Foxes', p. 26

Terrie O'Neill: 'Black Pig', p. 37; 'Cúchulainn', p. 92; 'Molly Weston', p. 130

Brian Power: "Death of Diarmait', p. 59; 'Al and Fairy', p. 83; 'Name of Delvin', p. 96; 'Garrawog', p. 99; 'Long Man', p. 121; 'Buried Alive', p. 133

Bobby Redmond: 'St Ultán', p. 67; 'Cursing of Tara', p. 86

Andrew Smyth: 'Dead Coach', p. 124